*This book is dedicated to the Late Shel Silverstein: author of The Giving Tree, who described his story this way: "It's just a relationship between two people. One gives and the other takes." Shel, may people **stop** using your poignant story to promote the "virtues" of self-debasement and personal sacrifice. May they stop coercing our children into same. May The Giving Stump make obvious these rampant, blatant bastardizations that promote conformity, indoctrination, and soullessness—everything you stood against in your musical, soulful and beautiful barefoot life.*

The Giving Stump

...the rest of the story

This book is for educational purposes only. It is not intended as a substitute or replacement for psychological, psychiatric, or any mental health care, nor is it intended to offer any mental health diagnosis or relationship advice, either explicitly or implicitly. Interpretation of the material can vary greatly by reader. This book is the author's expressed opinion only. She and the publisher are not responsible for how you interpret this information and you agree not to hold either liable. Further, the author is not a psychologist, psychiatrist, psychotherapist, neuroscientist, lawyer, medical doctor, life-coach, or any other medical, legal, or mental health practitioner and assumes no liability for your interpretation of the material herein, or any subsequent reaction, action, inaction you take in response to reading this book.

While every conceivable effort has been made to give accurate and verifiable information, this book does not give, nor should it be construed to give professional psychological, psychiatric, medical, or legal advice. If you need any type of advice, consult area-specific licensed professionals in your area. This book can challenge your current beliefs about love, relationships, romance and personal boundaries; it can prompt mild to severe emotional discomfort. The reader (or anyone to whom this book is read) assumes full responsibility for his or her unique interpretation of and subsequent reaction to the material in this book. If you experience overwhelming emotions or a sense of helplessness or despair, contact a local crisis center or other qualified crisis professional. If you need counseling or emergency shelter, seek out services from a local agency. If you feel suicidal, call 911 or a suicide / crisis hotline.

suicidepreventionlifeline.org / National Crisis Number:1-800-273-8255 TTY: 1-800-799-4889

Mentally ill people can be dangerous. Some can become verbally toxic, physically violent, and life-threatening when confronted / challenged. If you choose to leave an abusive relationship, seek help from a qualified mental health professional, crisis center, or local law enforcement. In life threatening emergencies, call 911. Neither the author nor this book offer advice on leaving or staying in any relationship. This is solely the reader's choice and responsibility.

Note: THE GIVING STUMP IS NOT A CHILDREN'S BOOK.

Copyright: Laurel Lee Cozzuli: October 10, 2018
Laurel Lee Publications & A Laurel Production
Written, edited and illustrated by Laurel Lee Cozzuli, MC
Cover design by Laurel Lee Cozzuli, MC
Produced and Printed in the U.S.A.
ISBN: 978-0-578-40160-7

A Laurel Production

If somebody corrupts the core of your being and your sense of reality, if somebody causes you to believe, 'Look, love isn't real. Humans aren't compassionate and caring; they're predatory monsters who will take your love and leverage that love against you, torture you, even unto death...' Now, for people who have not been in narcissistically abusive relationships, (who) don't know what Complex PTSD is, they'll say, 'That's overly dramatic. Nobody's getting tortured. You're not being tortured to death...' Well, shut the fuck up; you don't know what you're talking about. Unless you've been through it, you do not know what it is, and you cannot speak. This is not your terrain. You shouldn't be here."

~Richard Grannon, SpartanLifeCoach
YouTube: Effects of Narcissistic Abuse

Contents

thegivingstump.com

Gender and Narcissism

The statistics for narcissism shows a slightly higher tendency in males. However, both men and women (and everyone in-between) can be narcissists (or embody mental health conditions that mimic narcissism). Further, both males and females (and every-one in-between) are vulnerable to such abuse. In keeping with the characters in the story of The Giving Stump, I refer to the abuser as *he* and victim as *she*. These references are consistent throughout this book and discussion sections. This is for simplicity only.

Why the swearing in this book?

The swear words used in this book are purposeful and not due to a lack of couth or ignorance on the author's part. Most concerning to some readers is the use of the "c-word" by Boy near the end of the story. Boy's use of this mortifying insult is followed by he and Stump's dialogue about it, demonstrating how far a narcissist will go in efforts to manipulate his victim. Unbeknownst to Stump, his furtive goals are 1) getting her to believe and agree that he *didn't mean anything by it,* and 2) getting her to take the blame for him insulting her with "the c-word" in the first place. Ludicrous goals? Clearly. However, due to the stranglehold he has on Stump's life, Boy accomplishes them in very short order. Exploring these deception tactics within the context of this book can save you the agony of trying to navigate them in real life – should they ever show up. If you are involved with a narcissist, they very likely will.

Preface

The Giving Stump was written in response to the late Shel Silverstein's beloved 1964 classic, The Giving Tree. Through Shel's genius tale of epic ambiguity, the reader is left to ponder whether Tree's actions of giving the boy all of her apples, branches and trunk are altruistic and loving? Or self-debasing and enabling? The Giving Stump takes Tree's generous and loving inclinations toward her thankless, self-centered partner - and runs with them.

For the purpose of this book, Boy (who was closer to a 95 year old man in The Giving Tree) has been "de-aged" to a robust 65-70 year old. I chose to do this because he needs the strength and fire to pull off his manipulative stunts. I couldn't work this into a dialogue with a 90-something year old.

The Giving Stump contains typical narcissistic dialogue and behaviors that occur between the abuser and the abused. From the first page, it escorts the reader into the heart and soul of narc abuse, for the sole purpose of raising awareness. All of this is done through a silly relationship between a man and his tree stump.

Narcissistic abuse has become a catch-all phrase for much of the garden-variety abuse in society. This statement isn't meant to trivialize it, but to nod to the grim reality that you knew what I meant by "garden-variety abuse." This also forces a trivialization of narcissism – which, by the way, is a trait– not a diagnosis[1]. The result is that society is currently faced with a widespread, yet hidden and exponentially growing problem, with very few simple, practical, ways to identify it, stop it, and transform it.

Further, **narcissistic abuse is rarely obvious.** The best way to spot narcissistic abuse is by carefully observing the possible **victim**. Symptoms include: exhaustion, nervousness, adrenal fatigue, feeling invisible, inability to gain traction in life, brain fog, despondency (a gaunt or empty look in the eyes), hyper-startle response, hypervigilance, nightmares, insomnia, a sense of help-lessness, lack of confidence, isolation from friends and family, the onset or worsening of substance abuse, suicidal ideation, agoraphobia, self-loathing, self-negating, inability to describe why s/he feels so confused, angry or stuck, acting odd or eccentric, the onset of habits that are odd for the person, being overly accommodating and overly apologetic, and an inability to pinpoint or articulate the abuse they have endured.

If you recognize these symptoms in someone, be a critical thinker. Don't let a potential narcissist triangulate you against a victim. The process of getting out of an abusive relationship is a difficult, sometimes dangerous process. Abusers are conniving and vindictive, with self-serving agendas; they are skilled in convincing others that their **own** pathology exists within their victim(s).

---

[1] This information is from Dr. Ramani Durvasula, a psychologist and expert on narcissism.

Laurel Lee Cozzuli

Laurel Lee is comprehensively trained in various clinical trauma healing techniques and protocols. She worked for eight years as a mental health therapist in Arizona, USA. Most of her clients were victims of sexual assault, violent crime, narcissistic abuse, and domestic violence. She has extensively studied and practiced (and continues to study and practice) energy psychology techniques, life-transformational practices and spiritual healing methodologies. She is a Reiki Master through Sunlight Alliance[2] and a Divine Healing Hands Soul Healer through the Institute of Soul Healing and Enlightenment[3]. As a (now recovered and thriving) victim of narcissistic abuse, she is optimistic about the recent merging of the mental health and spiritual healing fields overall. She knows, first hand, that healing and thriving after narcissistic abuse requires an integrated, holistic approach.

Her unyielding views on strong interpersonal boundaries and healthy relationships spring from not only her hard-knock sentience gleaned as a victim, but also as a clinical therapist and a spiritual practitioner. Her stark writing style demystifies and exposes the typical slippery trickeries of narcissistic abuse that would otherwise remain hidden to most.

---

[2] https://sunnydawnjohnston.com/sunlight-alliance-foundation/
[3] https://www.drsha.com/

*In spite of her heartfelt dedication to spiritual principles of forgiveness, love and compassion, Laurel is an emphatic voice **against** the blanket "forgive and forget" practices that are taught by most religious and spiritual doctrines today. When it comes to healing powerless emotional trauma, blanket forgiveness practice often reinforce entrenched cycles of abuse, and, sadly, fortify the power differential between the abuser and the abused. Instead, Laurel teaches an integrated and psychologically sound approach to forgiveness: one that pairs healthy interpersonal boundaries with physical, emotional, mental and spiritual congruence.*

In 2012, Laurel tearfully walked away from her counseling licensure and career as a therapist after discovering (the hard way) indisputable evidence of rampant narcissistic abuse at her place of work: a prominent mental health agency in Arizona, as well as the morbidly corrupt Arizona Board of Behavioral Health Examiners. Completely broken, she turned her focus to her own healing. She soon began writing to educate the masses on the red flags, dangers and symptoms of covert mental and emotional abuse – not just in familial and partner relationships, but also its prevalence in the workplace. She also detailed the complex trauma and lifelong consequences that often result from being targeted and victimized by a narcissist or other bonafide bully.

The Giving Stump is the first in a series of four books that takes readers through the throes of recognizing, surviving, healing and thriving after narcissistic abuse.

Introduction

(Please read - important!)

You are about to be schooled - by a tree stump and her misfit beau.

The process of writing this book was demanding for me on many levels. First, it forced me to own up to my personal experiences of narcissistic abuse, what it has cost me, and the lengths I have gone to in order to heal from it. Second, over the years, I've developed an aversion to the word *victim*. I, like many of you, have heard the adages: *we are NOT victims of abuse, but willing participants and creators of our own lives and circumstances. There's no such thing as a victim. We choose everything that comes into our lives. Identifying yourself as a victim gives away your power. Yada yada yada...*

If you've done any form of personal growth or spiritual work, you've probably heard these adages a time or two. However true these truths are on a metaphysical level, like all things pure and holy, they are very often wielded in a way that absolves an abuser of responsibility for his actions. If you're like me, you have felt at least a little bit invalidated, confused and resentfully wedged into this notion that another person's abusive behaviors are on **you**. Hold up... isn't *blaming the victim* a hallmark of narcissism? *Hmm...*

My third challenge was in writing the *teasing apart the crazy* section of this book. At times, I was so outraged in trying to untangle

Boy's hidden manipulations that I became physically ill; I often needed to do EFT[4] and *therapize* myself through it. It dug into my own hidden woundedness. It stung. It unraveled me. It left me vulnerable, anxious and raw. Yet, I persevered. The process was ultimately insightful and empowering. I realized how much I now truly understand about narcissism and its heinous effects on humans - and that it must be exposed in truth. Being able to bring this knowledge to others has been worth every pang, every fear, every tear that has trickled down my face as my fingers flew over my keyboard and exposed the truth of this *beast in angel's clothing*. It's as if every word of The Giving Stump has triumphantly yanked a bit of my soul back from the vacuous bellies of the starving ones.

Okay... that's a little dramatic. But really, it fits. Narcissists are starving black holes with fabricated morals. They are takers. They voraciously suck life force energy from others through any means possible. They don't play by **any** rules – societal or personal. If you do set rules – explicitly or implicitly – they will bend them, break them, ignore them, change them as needed, for they believe their own agendas are far more important than any stupid rule.

Breaking free from my narc-vortices has meant everything for me. I went from drowning in spiritual sludge and fawning after the lie, to recognizing the zombie-con, to shaking free from it, and, finally, thriving in the sovereignty to be 100% me. Life is **so much better**

---

[4] *EFT stands for Emotional Freedom technique and involves gently tapping on pressure points.*

when you don't worry about what other people think of you. Who knew? It's like – living for real.

My dear reader, perhaps you've accepted your indefinable rut as a way of life. Perhaps you're living under suppositions and conditions that you've never even questioned. A fish doesn't know it's in water. A victim doesn't know she's in narcissist soup. Fortunately, you'll figure out very quickly if you've ever been a victim or not through the process of reading this book. How will you know? Well, you'll probably end up getting really pissed off. (Um… sorry? And you're welcome.)

Anger is villianized in most therapeutic and spiritual circles by the same geniuses who promote the notion *there's no such thing as a victim.* Anger misdirected is absolutely destructive. Yet, if utilized for its true purpose, anger becomes a crucial part of the personal healing and transformational journey. I will talk more on this concept in the next three volumes of The Stump Diaries series.

My final challenge in writing this book was this: there was seemingly no way for me to write it without ostensibly mocking or conveying judgment toward narcissists. This is a pretty big no-no in the emo-healing and spiritual zones today. Although, really, I'm *not* mocking or judging. I'm simply reporting the truth about narcissists. And they are so… pathetic underneath their attitudes and manipulations - it just *looks* like I'm mocking them.

I suppose I could have softened up my writing to appease those who toil over the need to squish and shape raw truth into affable and universally palatable empowerment widgets. I could also simply refer to *judgment* here as *discernment,* then gush about the deeper meaning of all the pain and devastation these heathens have caused me over the years. Then everybody would love me. They would say I'm *loving* and *nice* and *able to rise above* the behaviors of others and all that crap. Tempting, I tell ya!

Pffft.

No thanks. I've wasted far too much precious life force energy on such ignorant pursuits already. Also, I need to consciously guard against my inclination, as a recovering empath (aka: codependent) to squish around, reframe, and frantically work to extract my *life lessons* from other people's self-serving, twisted, and egotistical bullshit. There will be no squishing around of anything in this book. If you want squished spiritual stuff, go elsewhere. You can find more information about the dangers of spiritual squishing of narcissistic bullshit at SquishItAndDie.com. (Not really…)

The ugliness and dysfunction conveyed in this book is indicative of narcissism itself – and not my alleged judgment of it. All I did was write the truth about it. And out came *ugly.* (Who knew?) For my own sake (and yours) I needed to write this book as **truthfully and unambiguously** as possible, with nowhere for narcissists to hide, nothing for them to manipulate, and in an oratory that expresses the **reality** of what their manipulations actually look like... not what victims want them to be. I know it looks like I'm poking fun at narcissists. But I'm really not. Well, I guess I am... a little. But this, too, is purposeful, for laughing at the narcissist disempowers him and empowers his victims.

My goal with The Giving Stump is to bring into focus the **reality** of narcissistic abuse – not deliver some meaningless hippie-dippy dance around it. God knows we have enough of those books on the market. Eventually, yes, the spiritual lessons emerge, and you will see, with grace and gratitude, why you've been through such terrible experiences. But you will never authentically get there without first figuring out who you are without the approval of others. You will never get there until you take your power back and are able to protect yourself from further exploitation. You will not be able to take one step toward grace and gratitude without first seeing the fangs of the invisible beast you've been fighting.

My fellow free-loving tree huggers and spiritual dwellers: I respect you. I adore you. I get you. Please... don't rebuff my seemingly audacious points here. They are far too important to whitewash. For now, we call out the truth of this conniving brute in clear and present language. In this book, we own the reality of what he has cost us. And, occasionally, we laugh at him.

Is my approach spiritual? Geesh… who knows? Either way, something feels right on with it. There will be people, including in my own spiritual circles, who will raise eyebrows while reading this book. They may tell me that it's *harsh* and *judgmental*, and that I've created *bad karma* by writing it. Yet, before now, what have I accomplished by NOT? What have I accomplished these past eight years by cowering in my own pathetic-ness and hiding out in my surrogate spiritual sanctuaries? Secretly waiting for my abusers to fess up to their *mistakes*, make them right by the world, and finally set me free from their pervasive and enduring lies? What has been the benefit of me not standing up to and telling the truth about what *really happened* to my once joyful and thriving life? Remember my good reader: thou shalt not create chicken-shit karma. I'm pretty sure that's a thing.

At this juncture in my life I have the unique ability to bring others this much needed awareness through my experience as both a former trauma therapist and a survivor and thriver of narcissistic abuse. It's as if I've been spiritually called to radical authenticity. Therefore, in this book, I do NOT identify *problems* as *challenges*. I do not identify *pain* as *feedback*. I don't categorize *abusers* as *teachers* or *victims* as *participants*. For the love of God, People! Victims are confused enough. Our pain has been minimized and perverted enough. And certainly, this matter has been convoluted enough by the gaslighting, projection, and deflections going on at the very heart of it. I can't, in good conscience, contribute to this narc-web by using potentially confusing, sugar-coating jargon that will only serve to confuse the people I'm seeking to reach.

In spite of its harshness, this book was, indeed, divinely inspired. Had I written it in some reverent, *oh, look at how pious I am... do I have your approval?* style I would have been disgusted with it. Obviously, such an inauthentic approach to anything is a total waste of everything.

I know what this book would have meant to **me** eight years ago. Do you have **any** idea how many psychology webinars, self-healing colloquiums and sappy-happy-flower-power books I read trying to fix my three-ring-shit-show life? Exactly 853. Not a single one of them came close to fixing what the real problem was: that I was unknowingly being narcissistically abused in multiple areas of my life. Bugger!

While I recognize that all of that was, indeed, my path, it's also why I wrote this book exactly the way I did. I didn't need another psychology class, meme of wisdom, or esoteric spiritual passage to figure out why my life had stalled out in a steaming pile of hippo dung. What I needed was to **understand** what I was actually up against, and why I couldn't get a grip on anything substantial. Once I figured it out, I did what Laurel does: I owned it and dove directly into it (within myself – not by confronting or wailing on my abusers) in order to find and heal the hurt, broken, buried and wounded parts of me that were making me susceptible to this nasty abuse in the first place. Only then did my 853 whatevers mean anything substantial and applicable in my life.

This profound life transformation - it's just too good not to share. In order to accomplish my mission of helping as many people as I can who are suffering in the same way, I needed a narcissistic **storyline** to reference... one that exemplified the raw truth about covertly abusive dialogue, delivered in a straightforward, palatable and quasi-goofy way. I couldn't find one. So I wrote one. Then I analyzed the hell out of it and put it all into a book. Voila! The Giving Stump. *Meep-meep!*

By the way, yes, eventually, ***forgiving*** your abusers (authentically forgiving – not wet-blanket or guilt-induced-forgiving) will be *muy importante* for your transformation and personal peace. There is no contradiction here. Forgiveness doesn't mean you tolerate abusive relationships. Rather, forgiveness is a state you hold in your own heart that frees you from the illusion of powerlessness. Forgiveness allows you to make decisions that are congruent with your truth.

Yet, true forgiveness can't happen if you're still trying to play nice with a tyrant. It can't happen if you're lying low, waiting for your abuser's tyrannical storms to pass. It' can't happen if you still subconsciously fear or resent *the takers,* or your spiritual abductors.

True forgiveness can't happen in a relationship that keeps you mentally vigilant. It can't happen if you are unwilling to own the truth of his demoralizing actions that satiate his wonky pathology. True forgiveness doesn't happen if you're still trying to navigate his mind games in fruitless pursuit of his understanding or love. True forgiveness can't happen if you're lost to his mania or are still pining away after his elusive approval. Once you really get this, your whole life and reality will radically shift.

There is something mystically powerful about an enlightened empath—meaning an empath who has been broken a by narcissist… and thrives to tell about it. An enlightened empath is a confident, integrated and cogent truth bearer. She sees and transcends the veiled manipulations of the *false gods*: the bedazzled personalities who reek of charisma, false charm and fabricated virtue… which, unannounced, callously morph into deception, crazy-making, and intimidation. An enlightened empath has the unique ability to strip away imaginary powers from the predatory souls who can only survive by manipulating and devouring the trusting, forgiving, fawning, and meek. The empowered empath is blessed with the divine authority to speak perfect truth with authentic love. She is esoterically immunized against the delusions of those who once heartlessly ruled her. And she somehow has the cheek to forgive the soul-sucking cretins to boot.

You want in? Your first step is to comprehend exactly what covert mental abuse looks like, feels like, sounds like, smells like, tastes like. While this isn't as fun as sticking your head in the sand or numbing out with wine, without comprehending the multi-layered, multi-faceted, and multi-level manipulation tactics of narcissistic abuse, any healing effort you take to fix your life will probably prove frustratingly futile. You need to know this tyrant inside and out if you ever hope to outsmart him. You need to know what makes you vulnerable to his attacks, and what needs to heal within you so you can protect yourself from such treatment in the future.

This first book in this series, *The Giving Stump: The Rest of the Story* is all about narcissistic abuse awareness. **Awareness** is a crucial first step in any healing journey, and one that is often skipped over in a victim's desperation to ease emotional pain. However nerve-wracking it may be for you, reading this book will empower you with knowledge and start you on your journey of reclaiming your precious, life-bearing soul. Such a journey is worth every pang, every fear, every tear that may trickle down your face as the truth is revealed to you, line by line.

In this light, my dear reader, I give to you, in all her exploited glory, The Giving Stump.

The Giving Stump:

the rest of the story

"You are a very hard stump," Boy said scornfully. He shifted his seat, trying to get comfortable. Stump felt her roots shiver with a familiar disparity. She thought of every way possible to make herself softer, but there's only so much **soft** that can be bamboozled out of yourself when you are a tree stump. Stump had no branches. therefore, she had no leaves to pillow his bony ol' butt... while he sat contemplating his miserable and cluster-fucked life.

She tried to think of happy things to talk about in order to distract him from his discomfort. "Boy, do you remember when I let you pick my apples so you could sell them? Did that make you happy?"

"Your apples?!" Boy curled his lip in disgust. "Good God, no, Stump! You know I didn't make a cent off those rotten, worm- riddled sacs."

Stump's heart dropped and thumped heavily. She was dumbfounded. What was Boy saying about her precious and perfect apples? They were rotten? Worm riddled? Preposterous! "Um... Boy? Uh... you're mistaken. My apples were neither rotten nor worm-riddled." she spoke gently but firmly, just like she had been taught in her self-assertiveness training. "They most certainly were!" Boy barked back.

Stump jumped at Boy's abrupt comeback. Her heart thumped. She was stumped. Perhaps Boy was just confused. Her apples were wonderful and delicious. She wouldn't have given them to him if they weren't.

Her baby apples were very dear to her. She had given them to Boy out of the goodness of her heart so he would know how much she loved him. For these many years, the only thing that gave her comfort over the loss of her beautiful apples was the knowing that Boy had made money selling them - to hungry people who were nourished by their deliciousness.

"You should be grateful I took those appalling apples off your hands," he said flatly. "They shouldn't even be called apples. They should be called appalls." Boy gave a snarky laugh. "Get it? Because they were so appaaaalllling?" Boy belly-laughed and snorted.

Stump didn't answer him for holding back her tears. She hoped Boy wouldn't notice how upset she was; that never went well.

"HellooooOOO?" Boy jeered. "What? You're not going to answer me or laugh at my jokes now? How rude!"

Stump remained silent for fear of crying. She had grown her apples from tiny buds. She nourished and doted on them for an entire season. She raised them to be upstanding, healthy apples. When Boy picked them, she was giving him a very dear piece of herself.

Strangely, the mere thought of her apples being rotten and wormy brought up feelings of deep shame This made defending her apples positively gut-wrenching!

Stump desperately wanted to correct Boy's very faulty memory of her apples. "Boy," her voice quivered, "many people have

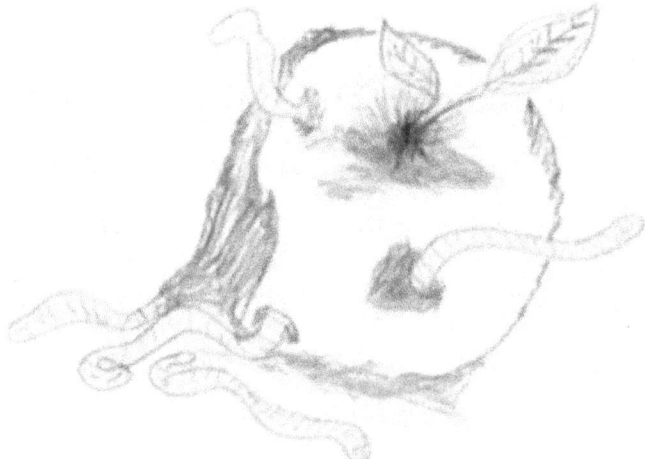

told me that my apples were extremely delicious and juicy. I don't understand why you would say..."

"You know those people were all lying to you," Boy interrupted her. "They felt sorry for you because, obviously, you're a bit pathetic. You know I always tell you the truth, even if it hurts."

What Boy didn't tell Stump is this: he actually made a killing off her apples. It just wasn't enough money to pay off his massive gambling debts. So technically, he wasn't lying. Plus, he only gambled because Stump was such an annoying nag. He needed to distract himself from her infernal yammering. Therefore, obviously, his debt was all her fault.

Stump didn't speak for several minutes. She was twisted in angst, trying to make sense of Boy's ludicrous account of her beloved apples. How on earth could he remember her decadent and delicious apples as being rotten and wormy? And was she REALLY pathetic? Were all those people REALLY lying to her? None of this made any sense! But Boy... he was her soulmate. He would never lie to her...

Stump finally decided to be the bigger person and just let it go... and avoid any further argument. She knew that the best approach to this silly misunderstanding was unconditional love and forgiveness.

She was in love with Boy! They needed each other. She knew he would be so very lost without her! Boy had suffered a terrible childhood, which is why he behaved like this. She knew that she was put in his life to help him break through the walls he had built around his heart. She couldn't let this pettiness get in the way of her mission to rescue him from himself.

"I would grow you more apples, Boy," Stump said lovingly. "Better, more delicious apples. But... do you remember? I gave you my branches to build a house."

Boy gave Stump a look of indifference. He shifted his gaze back to the ground. "God, my butt hurts."

"Tell me about your house, Boy..." Stump said, trying to again distract him from his uncomfortable sit.

"Oh, God. Why? You know a storm took that piece-of-crap-shack from me long ago. Your wood was porous and weak. I should have known you'd give me bad wood to build my house."

"Whaaaat?! You lost my branches?!" Stump blurted in horror.

"Oh, brother. Here we go! Always gotta be nagging at me for something."

"But those were my branches, Boy! I needed them to make leaves and apples!"

"Then why did you give them to me?!"

"Because you needed a house! And I love you, Boy!"

"Well you sure don't act like it!" Boy retorted. "Don't you get it?! I lost my house. I became homeless. Because your branches sucked and you knew it. You wanted to get rid of them and offloaded them onto me."

Stump was in utter disbelief. *Offload them onto him? How could he possibly say that? Her branches were a* tremendous gift to Boy. She missed them terribly. Her life had become grueling since giving them to him. She no longer had leaves to soak up the sun, produce chlorophyll, change colors in the fall, or dance in summer gale. It was an awful thing to be a tree with no leaves. Or branches. The only thing that gave her comfort was knowing that Boy had built a beautiful, sturdy house with them and was enjoying the comforts of his own home, which was built with the superb wood she so lovingly gave him.

"I had to move into my parents' basement after it fell down." Boy jeered. "I wish you hadn't brought up such a terrible memory, Stump."

Stump, again, felt deeply ashamed, even though she knew Boy wasn't remembering the truth about her wood. She didn't offload anything onto him! He had asked her, rather desperately actually, if she could give him a house. She didn't have a house, but generously offered him her branches in order that he may build one. How was Boy not remembering any of this correctly? Also, he had never told her about his house falling down or needing to move into his parents' basement. So how could she have known not to mention it?

Boy continued. "You talk a good game, Stump. But all you ever do is twist the knife with your, 'oh boo hoo, Boy! Those were my branches!' Why would you even say something like this to me, Stump? That was my house." Boy's voice cracked with emotion – a skill he had been able to perfect over the years. Fooling Stump into believing she was the one who was being insensitive would win this argument. Booyaahh! It worked. Stump instantly felt like shit, and had no rebuttal.

Stump felt dreadful about making Boy sad. Maybe she really was being selfish? He was obviously upset about his house falling down. Who wouldn't be? Maybe this was why he was blaming her for giving him bad wood. But... gosh! This was sheer absurdity! She knew her wood was of excellent quality. She reminded herself that Boy had a difficult childhood and she needed to cut him some slack. He was her soulmate, after all. They had a very powerful soul connection. In spite of how he acted, she knew he loved her too. She just knew it.

Stump knew that her only choice was to forgive him and let it go. It really wasn't THAT big of a deal... right? When she calmed herself down and was able to swallow her truth to a manageable level, she spoke. "Boy, I care about you so much! Please forgive me for not giving you good wood."

Boy shrugged. "Don't worry about it. It's in the past." Although he would never, EVER admit it, Boy absolutely knew that Stump's wood was extremely sturdy and strong. In fact, at the time, Boy couldn't believe his good fortune... that Tree would just GIVE him ALL of her branches! Especially after he had been such a jerk to her! After she gave him all her apples, he just dumped her without any explanation. That was great fun! She kept calling him and being all sweet... trying to figure out what she did wrong.

Of course, he never gave her any explanation as to why he didn't come around anymore. This made her *freak out* and get desperate. Predictable. *yawn!* Her desperation came in handy though! He was able to get her branches off her for nothing! Of course, his stunning good looks had something to do with it. Women couldn't resist him, and he secretly knew it. This chick, Stump, was so desperate for his approval that she would do ANYTHING to get it. Obviously, Boy would have been a total fool not to capitalize on this opportunity.

The real problem with building his house was that Boy didn't really know what he was doing. He was obviously too smart to follow the dumb ol' directions. Once he was done, his house looked like it was built by a band of monkeys who had escaped the clutches of a maniacal zoo keeper... and happened upon a random pile of logs, a jar of peanut butter, and a hammer.

Now, in Boy's defense, he had run out of nails half-way through building his house. Because of the yammering wooden wench annoying him while he was cutting off her branches, he ended up spending all of his money that night gambling. Thus, he had no money to buy more nails. He ended up using peanut butter and kite string to hold the rest of the logs together. He cleverly propped up the sagging west wall with a toilet plunger. It worked great!

Directions my ass! He cracked open a beer and stepped back to admire his handiwork. Regrettably, using all his peanut butter and plunger to stabilize his house would temporarily put a damper on he and Stella's bedroom romps. Yet, he fully intended to buy nails the next day so he could finish the job correctly. He was good like that.

Then... he kinda-sorta forgot all about it. A couple weeks later, a gusty thunderstorm came along and obliterated his house. *Motherfucker!!! Damn that yammering Tree and her stupid crap wood!* Sadly, his plunger was washed away in the torrential rain that fateful day too. *FACK!*

Stump felt bad that Boy had lost his home. Although it was terribly distressing that Boy didn't remember her wood as high quality and strong, she felt his pain. She pressed the subject gently, hoping he might soften up a bit and she could remind him of the truth about her branches... how much unconditional love she had showed him by giving them to him! Surely he would see it. Right now, more than anything, he needed to know he was loved. "Boy, you know it took me more than 25 years to slowly grow my wood..."

"I said don't worry about it!" Boy said gruffly. Obviously, he was doing Stump a huge favor by letting it go. (What a guy... What a guy...)

Stump sighed and fell silent. She had intentionally grown her wood slowly, pulling nourishment from Mother Earth and the sun... for the better part of a quarter-century in order to grow her strong wood. But Boy would never see it or listen to reason. He only ever saw things from his point of view, which was usually skewed in some tenuous way that made her look bad.

Maybe she had missed something? Maybe her wood really **was** porous and weak? She mustn't be so arrogant to think it was high quality and strong. She would let this conversation go too, out of her love and devotion to Boy, and her commitment to being a good person. After a few minutes, she spoke again, hoping to change the mood to a lighthearted one. She knew just what to say. "Hey... Boy? My wood was porous, so my trunk must have made a fine and buoyant boat. Right?"

"Jesus! Heck no, Stump! That was actually the worst boat ever. I mean, I carved it perfectly, of course. But your trunk was weak and full of air pockets. We tried to sail to an island and it hit a jagged rock. Knocked a hole clean through it. You should have told me your wood wasn't strong enough to be a thin-hulled boat."

"Whaaaaat??!!" Stump felt like a sharp rock had just been slammed through her heart! In a way, it had. "What? My... your... my... your... boat sunk???!!" She was barely able to express her spinning thoughts, as she frantically tried to mentally process what had happened to her precious, perfect trunk. She felt like she had been punched in the heart by a gorilla. She tried, but she couldn't hold in her tears. She softly sobbed as she spoke, "That was my only trunk, Boy! Don't you understand that I gave it to you out of the goodness of my heart?" Boy remained silent. He held no expression on his face, save a hint of a smile in his eyes. "Why didn't you tell me about this when it happened, Boy? I think I deserved to know what happened to my trunk..."

"God! Stop yelling!" Boy sneered.

What-what? She wasn't yelling! What is he even talking about? "What? I'm not yelling, Boy!" Stump raised her voice, but still wasn't yelling.

"You're yelling while saying you're not yelling?!" Boy asserted scornfully.

"I'm talking louder now because you're accusing me of something I'm not doing!"

"Talking louder is yelling!" He yelled. "You accuse me of all kinds of shit, but you can't own up to yours? How does that make any sense, Stump?"

Stump couldn't take much more of this. Boy refused to listen to her and made everything her fault! She decided to just shut up, because everything she ever said just made matters worse.

But she loved Boy! She needed to figure this out! If he would only listen to her for a minute and stop making such ridiculous assumptions...

"Jesus Christ. If you must know, I didn't tell you about your trunk sinking because I didn't want you to feel guilty for putting our lives in danger. You know, it's your responsibility to warn people if your wood is low quality. Instead, you sold me on it like some snake-oil salesman."

"What in the heck are you talking about?!" Stump's

sadness turned to fury. "I GAVE YOU MY WOOD AS A GIFT!" Now, Stump WAS yelling... much to Boy's delight. "So you could get away from all of your problems! I didn't sell you on anything!"

"God! Chill out already! You always get so dramatic over nothing."

"This isn't nothing, Boy! You're telling me my trunk was nothing? You're not even grateful for it! And now you're saying I should feel GUILTY for giving it to you? And it's somehow MY fault that YOU almost drowned? When you're the klutz who wrecked it?"

"I know it's hard for you to understand, even short sentences, I guess..." Boy spoke with an exaggerated tone of authority, as if Stump was the stupidest person on the planet for believing what she was saying... which was actually the truth. "But if you would LISTEN— I said I DIDN'T want you to feel guilty, which is why I never told you about the boat sinking. Why do you ALWAYS twist things around?"

"Are you kidding me? You stupid fucker! How dare

you blame me for that?! Fuck you! Fuck YOU!!!" Her anger was surging, and she couldn't exactly explain why. All she knew was that Boy was being grossly unfair and outrageously ignorant. As usual!

"God, you're bipolar, Stump." Boy jeered. How dare this pathetic, whiny, worthless stump question him?! It seems like someone needed a reality check as to who was the boss in this relationship! "Look, Little Miss Can-Do-No-Wrong, I'm the victim here. I trusted you, and it nearly cost me my life! Your trunk sunk so fast we almost got sucked down with it! Stella and I needed to leap for our lives and swim to the island! So don't you dare blame me, Stump!"

"Boy! My trunk was not crap, and you know it!"

"You're so arrogant! How would you know if your trunk was crap or not? I'm the one who carved it into a boat — not you. And I can tell you for sure that your trunk was weak, full of air pockets, and made a horrible boat. Which is why it rammed into a rock and instantly sunk to the bottom of the ocean!"

Stump was beside herself with anger and grief. Boy had a way of making these sweeping junk statements that were so far-fetched; there was just no way to form a rebuttal against them. Like so many other times, his statements weren't adding up. "Boy!" she yelled much louder than she intended to. "You're full of it! If my wood was porous and full of air pockets, it would NOT have sunk so fast!"

Crap. He hadn't thought of that. Not to worry; he knew how to shut her down: inconsequential blame and tangential discussion... meaning discussion that sounds like he's addressing the issue but he's really just talking around it. He had spent years perfecting his craft, and it had gotten him out of a lot of really bad situations where he would have otherwise had to take responsibility.

"Geeesh! You can't let anything go, can you?! Don't ask me to figure out your crazy wood growth! I don't know why your wood sunk so fast. All I know is I did you a HUGE favor by taking that crappy trunk off your hands. So you wanna shut your pie hole and stop calling me a liar?"

Stump saw no way through Boy's delusional and twisted convictions that made her out to be the irrational one and absolved him of responsibility. He shoved his twisted accounts of her beautiful and by-gone trunk, along with blame for HIS irresponsibility and recklessness in her face.

Stump couldn't tell if he really believed his delusions? Or if he was just making them up as he went along? Nothing about Boy ever made sense. Sometimes she wished she had never met him.

Several silent minutes passed. She was beyond angry and doing her best to breathe through it.

She kinda knew that she had pressed the issue about her sunken trunk too far. And she felt horrible about dropping the f-bomb. She also knew that, because of Boy's abysmal childhood, he didn't know how to take responsibility, and he couldn't help being the way he was. Therefore, she really had no choice but to forgive him and let it go.

Yet... Stump missed her trunk very much, and she

just couldn't pretend that she didn't. She was deeply hurt, confused, and frustrated; it was getting harder and harder to rationalize away his behavior. *Ugh. Relationships are hard!*

Before today, she had comforted herself with the belief that Boy was enjoying his time sailing away from all his problems... in her trunk that she had so lovingly gave him.

What hurt Stump even more was that she knew Boy's soul was in deep trouble. It was obvious by his delusions and behaviors that something was really wrong with him, and it was her job to help him.

While most other women probably rejected him, Stump knew she was special. She had always been able to forgive and love Boy through all of it, and show him that he DOES matter, that he IS loveable, and that she would ALWAYS be there for him. She needed to help him. God had put her in his life so she could help him, because he never had the love he needed as a child. She could give him that love. She was committed to loving him **no matter what**.

She didn't share these thoughts with friends or family anymore. They were all angry with her and held so much judgment toward him! No one understood her deep love for Boy. It's true that Boy was horrid to her most of the time. She knew she tolerated a lot from him. And at times she wondered WHY she still loved him? Sometimes Stump wished she could just get over him like everyone told her to. But she didn't know how.

Something else Boy said had the potential to break her heart even more than knowing her trunk was sleeping with the fishes. Stump took a deep breath. "Boy, who's Stella?"

"Stella? I don't know. Why?"

"You said you and Stella had to jump off the sinking boat and swim to the island…"

"I never said Stella."

"Yes you did, Boy. I heard you, loud and clear."

"No, I didn't. I said… Fella. Fella is my dog."

"You have a dog named Fella?"

"Yes, I have a dog named Fella. Open up your ears."

"And you took him on the boat to an island?"

"Yes!" Boy raised his voice. "Yes! Why is this such a complicated subject? I took my dog on the crap boat with me to the island. I find it unbelievable that I just told you I almost drowned in the sea and my dog had to drag me to shore and island natives had to revive me and all you can do is ask about the name of my dog! What on earth is wrong with you?! Are you PMS-ing or something?"

Whuuuut did he just say? That he almost drowned? Then insinuated she didn't care? Then accused her PMS-ing? What? Just... what??

Stump was, again, faced with a whirlwind of non-sense that she felt powerless to counter. There was nothing to do here but forgive it and let him know she cared. "I'm sorry, Boy... I didn't hear you say that you almost drowned..."

"I said it! But you never listen!" Boy retorted.

Stump sighed. Boy was just being his impossible self again. Sadly, it was nothing she hadn't witnessed or forgiven before. But Boy really was so angry and convicted about all this... so he must be telling the truth... from his warped perspective. *Maybe he is just this confused? Maybe he really thinks I don't care that he almost drowned? But... he knows better!* There were so many unanswered questions, and she never seemed to get any straight answers. Maybe if she spoke very gently, he would listen. "Boy, I've missed you so much... and I don't remember you ever saying you had a dog named Fella... or that you almost drowned... and I just want you to be honest with me about Stella..."

"Oh, quit your yammering, Stump! I'm sick of you going on and on and on with nonsense. We've talked about this for 20 minutes. Can we be done with it?"

"But Boy, you didn't answer any of my..."

"PLEASE??!!" He yelled gruffly, as if he was very put

out. Stump fell silent.

Boy went on a self-pitying rant of embittered grumbling. "Mrfsgegerf damn it... hermb ererergerm eferber...I haven't ererergermeseen you in fermescur years rmererergermefe....I'm rmescuhalf hour and you're hermedederbrrmehjerscreby back to rmescu same incessant nagging. I jererergermefet here and have a nice rest rmescu spend time with you, ererergermefe ruin the peace and quiet mescur bederme foot-stool wannabe..."

Stump said nothing. This was maddening, unfair, and awful! Yet she had faith that Boy would one day break through his anger and see who she really was: a kind, forgiving, supportive person who loved him with her whole heart.

Truth be told, she was actually a little desperate. Nobody else would want her at this point. She had no apples, no leaves, no branches, no trunk... she had given all of these things up to this man she loved. God had put her in charge of saving Boy's soul, so giving him everything that ever meant anything to her was part of the rumble. She mustn't question it.

In spite of all of her flaws, and the fact that he was so mad at her all the time, she knew Boy loved her very much. She was worried about him. He was so fragile and always had such terrible things happen to him. Like his house falling down and his boat sinking. **Of course** he blamed her; it wasn't safe to blame himself because of his bad childhood. Stump knew that he just could never make it in life without her unconditional love and support.

Stump couldn't bear the thought of him ever being with another woman. While it seemed he might have been, it was easier to just let it go and give the whole situation to God. She knew that she mustn't let her imagination get carried away with her on this Stella thing. He probably did say Fella. She just heard him wrong. Like always. She sighed. "I'm sorry, Boy."

"You get on my last nerve, Stump!" Boy lifted his hat and smoothed back his thinning salt-and-pepper hair. "Even Tom and Harry agree with me: that you're crazy and impossible!" He replaced his hat.

"Who... who are Tom and Harry?" She asked timidly.

"Tom and Harry! You know? The guys I play squash with. Jesus! You don't remember a thing, do you?"

Boy knew Stump would be mortified about Tom and Harry – who didn't actually exist. Distracting Stump with the idea of Tom and Harry was his best bet to get her off this Stella rant – which he, of course, had invoked on purpose. Later she would realize he never gave her a direct answer, and she would toss and turn all night because of it. Ha! Dumb bitch. *Oh yeah! Mega heartbreaker in da house, y'all!*

Stump was mortified that Boy told Tom and Harry that she was crazy and impossible! Why would he do that? She wasn't crazy OR impossible! She was nice! She was giving! She was kind! But Tom and Harry could only know what Boy had told them about her. How could she make this right? She knew that if she were able to talk to them, she could explain this misunderstanding. But she knew that Boy would never let her meet them. She never got to meet any of his friends.

What it all came down to was this: she needed to regain Boy's respect. But she wasn't sure how to do that. The only thing she could think of was that she needed to go on a really strict health kick to get her body back. A protein shake and daily exercise would help her regrow her trunk, branches, and apples. That way, she could give Boy more apples and wood. Then he'd be in love with her again. Yep! That's it. She'd start tomorrow.

A few years ago, she had decided to take her life-savings and get herself a trunk implant. She ended up canceling her surgery last minute and giving the money to Boy; he needed to buy a new car because his old one somehow ended up at the bottom of a lake. (Pooooor Boooyyy!!!) She needed to help him!

She finally heard him sigh and felt his bony butt relax. Thank God. It would be safe for her to speak again, as long as she didn't mention Tom, Harry, Stella, Fella, the boat, her apples, her branches, her trunk, or anything else that Boy might interpret as upsetting or weird.

Sadly, she couldn't think of a single thing to say.

But the silence was deafening! She needed to say SOMEthing! "Your... butt feels nice and relaxed, Boy."

"Huh?!" Boy lifted his head and furrowed his brow. What the... hell is that supposed to mean?"

Stump was embarrassed.

Actually, this was ridiculous. She was getting really tired of feeling this way. Truth be told, she was exhausted with this whole walking on eggshells bit that he had reduced her to... even though she didn't actually have feet. Heck, maybe her family and friends were right. Maybe she deserved better. Maybe Boy was just a grumpy, miserable old man who was using her during his dry spells. These thoughts hurt her heart. But Boy's attitude toward her was simply unbearable anymore. For the first time in a long time, she started to entertain the idea of ending their relationship. Stump went deep into thought, wondering how exactly she would tell him that she just couldn't see him anymore.

"Isn't this a pretty day?" Boy asked cheerfully, as if no awful, manipulative or degrading conversation had just taken place between them.

Huh? Stump was brought out of her deep thought by Boy's unexpected cheer. She finally responded. "Oh. Oh! Yes! It's so sunny!" She spoke in the happiest tone she could muster. She was grateful for Boy's change of mood. She knew this was because she was so forgiving, and he was finally breaking through all the pain around his heart. (Hallelujah! Praise Jesus!) "I love these crisp, sunny days with you, Boy."

"Yep! We've shared a lot of them together... 'ey Stump?" Boy gave her a pat.

"Indeed! We've had so many fun times, Boy." Stump was enjoying this unanticipated moment of nostalgia with him. She sighed deeply and smiled to herself. The love and faith in her heart quickly returned.

The sun was shining just for them in this moment. Ahh! The sweet sun! How she missed her leaves! And the days when she could bask its generous warmth and contribute to the precious oxygen stores on the planet, with Boy resting comfortably in her branches. These were some of the happiest memories of her life.

How silly of her to think that Boy was just a grumpy, miserable man who was using her during his dry spells. Nothing could be further from the truth. He loved her. And she loved him. This moment proved it.

Stump got a bit choked up on her feelings of the moment. Sadly, this caused her to speak without thinking. "Oh, Boy! I wish I still had my branches so you could climb up and hide in me and forget about the world." Stump stopped short, realizing she had just uttered words about a touchy subject: her branches. "Um... I mean..."

"God, you just had to bring it up again, didn't you?" Boy sneered.

"I'm sorry, Boy... I didn't mean it was your fault..."

"Whatever, Stump. You're always trying to make me

feel guilty for something. When are you going to face the facts? Your leaves are gone. Your apples are gone. Your branches are gone. Your trunk is gone. Just... friggin' deal with it! And stop making me out to be the tyrant in this relationship! God! Do you have any idea what I have to put up with from you?"

Stump felt scrambled and devastated. She strived to be the most loving, docile, easygoing person she could for him, but it wasn't easy. She knew that Boy couldn't help the way he was. He just couldn't. She needed to try harder to bite her tongue and extend compassion – and not get so angry with him. Poor guy. *I'm such a bitch!* Her heart sunk into shame.

How was it that she tried *so hard* to be his every-thing, yet she was constantly reduced to nothing? All of the beautiful parts of her were gone. She had given them to him, trying to make him happy. But no matter what she gave him, it wasn't enough, she was always messing up... and she was always empty.

Boy never apologized for hurting her feelings. Yet she was always apologizing to him – even for the stuff he did. She always tried like crazy to make things right.

Stump comforted herself with the pearls of wisdom she had heard from her wise elders over the years:

"Love means never having to say you're sorry."

"Unconditional love means we look past our loved one's flaws to their good underneath it."

"True love conquers all."

"All you need is love."

"Love is the answer."

Stump took a deep breath and told herself she was NOT giving up on Boy or their relationship.

"I'm hungry," said Boy. "I sure could go for an apple right now."

Stump slumped.

"Oh yeah..." Boy grumbled.

Boy sighed deeply. Several silent moments passed until he casually leaned back on his hands and crossed one foot over the other. He started to hum a cheerful tune: User Friendly, by Marilyn Manson. Stump was confused by his return to cheer, but grateful he was no longer angry with her.

Boy spoke in a happy tone. "It's so weird how you and I are actually dating. Don't you think, Stump?"

"Why? What do you mean, Boy?"

"I don't know," Boy said nonchalantly. "Maybe 'cuz I usually date women with bigger boobs and a nicer ass than you."

Stump was flabbergasted. "Boy, why would you even say such a mean thing to me?!"

"Huh? What? <insert dumb and confused look here.> I'm just saying that I usually date women with bigger boobs and a nicer ass. Why do you always have to take everything so personally?"

"I would never say something like that to you. That's so rude!"

"Oh, now I'm the rude one? Seriously, Stump? I thought you had better self-esteem than that. I can't even make a simple comment without you freaking out."

Once again Stump was angry and deeply hurt. Why would he even **think** to say something like this? Then not understand why she was upset? He must have been kicked in the head by a donkey or ran over by a rogue carpet cleaner as a kid. Any normal person would be able to SEE how hurtful this comment was. How did he not get it?!

She then wondered if, indeed, she *was* too sensitive and was freaking out over nothing? She just didn't know anymore. If she were to be really honest with herself, she knew she had let her body go over the last few years... to the point he may not be as attracted to her. Maybe this is just his way of trying to subtly drop the hint? She decided to forgive his misstep. He was probably right: she didn't need to take his comment personally.

A minute later, Boy stood up. "I need to take a dump, Stump. Can you give me a toilet?"

"Boy, I don't have a toilet. I'm a tree stump."

"Humph. What good are you, Stump?"

Stump felt ashamed by her lack of toilet-ness. "I'm sorry, Boy. I wish I could be better for you..." She knew Boy was getting ready to leave, and she would spend many lonely days waiting for his return. But she had no idea how to make him stay... or how give him something that she didn't have.

"I gotta walk a mile and a half up the road to take the browns to the super-bowl, Stump. If you want me to visit you more often, you need to get a toilet." He started to walk off.

"Boy, wait!" Stump cried.

"What now, Stump?"

"Um... I... um..." Stump stammered. "Well, Boy, maybe you... you can carve me into a toilet."

Boy stared at Stump in disbelief. His silence made her nervous.

"I mean... um...," she stammered. "If you want to, then you wouldn't need to walk so far to use the bathroom."

Boy brought his hand to his chin and con-templated Stump's odd proposition. Though he didn't lead on, he felt an excitement that she hadn't ignited in him in a long time.

The first time he felt this primal excitement was when she let him take her apples... after his "oh, boo hoo, Tree! I don't have any money!"

story. He thought THAT was a thrill. But then, she let him take her branches, which she was stupid enough to give up for him after his "boo hoo! I don't have a house!" story.

That excitement was only outdone by his "Oh, Tree! I'm so sad! I need to get away... in a boat!" story... and she let him cut down her trunk – a trunk that took her 25 years to grow – just so he could slam it into a jagged rock the first time he and Stella took it out on the water. HA! Stupid wench.

Stump had just handed him a golden ticket for the thrill of the century. This whole "you can carve me into a toilet" proposal was horrible, cruel and down-right disgusting... and far too good to pass up! "Well... shut my mouth, my Little Apple Tart! That's actually a great idea!"

"It... it is?"

"Yes! It is!" Boy pulled out his pocket knife. "You're brilliant! It's a very, very good idea!"

"Okay..." but Stump was suddenly unsure about it.

"Stump, if I carved you into a toilet, I could visit you every day," Boy spoke gently and assuredly.

"You could?" Stump asked, taken aback by Boy's sudden kindness. "Every day?"

"Yes! Because I wouldn't have to walk into town to use the bathroom."

Stump wanted, more than anything, to believe him. Boy had stopped visiting her every day a long, long time ago. Could this bathroom inconvenience be at the heart of his decision to stay away from her?

Deep down, Stump didn't believe Boy would really visit her every day, even if she let him carve her into a toilet. But she was so desperate that she would even settle for a once-a-week-after-a-six-pack-2-a.m. visit from him. But even that seemed like a tall order for Boy.

Yet, Boy was older now. Certainly, at this point in his life, he realized there wasn't another woman alive today who would love him as deeply as she did. Surely he realized that that life without love was not worth living at all. Surely he realized that Stump was the BEST thing that ever happened to him. Where else was he going to find someone even half as generous, kind, and loving as she was?

Boy loved having this much control over Stump. He could manipulate her into doing just about anything. Lately, she had become boring; there was very little left to exploit in her, thus very little left to feed his soul. But this? Literally carving her guts out? He was highly aroused just thinking about it. Just wait 'til the boys at the Titty-Tushy-Tavern hear about this!

Stump then caught sight of the pocket knife in Boy's hand. She shuddered. "Um Boy, you don't intend to use that tiny, dull knife to carve me – do you? That will hurt too much."

Ahh, crap. He was looking forward to slowly scraping away her insides using a dull knife. He wasn't used to resistance from her. The stumpy tramp! Time to up the ante.

"Oh, come on, baby! It won't be bad. I'll be gentle."

"No, Boy... you need to use a better knife."

Boy was miffed. He didn't have a better knife! Not with him. How dare she inconvenience him? Luckily, he knew just how to sway her resolve to his favor. "Stump..." boy's demeanor was suddenly solemn. "I've got a confession to make."

"What?" Stump was curious. "What is it?"

"I understand why you don't want me to use this dull knife. Even though it's the one my grand-daddy gave me from the Civil War... right... right before he died." Boy wiped an imaginary tear from his eye.

Huh? This was very strange talk coming from Boy. "You do??" Except in the beginning of their relation-ship, Stump never heard any form of understanding compassion, or sadness coming from him. *<insert twilight zone music here.>*

"Yes, my love. I know what it's like to have dull pain in your gut."

"Oh..." Stump's heart blipped with delight upon hearing him call her "my love." *swooon...*

"You see, the reason I haven't been able to visit you very much is because I have irritable bowel syndrome. I was diagnosed with it years ago, and, well, I need to be very near a bathroom at all times, or things could get messy."

"Oh no! Boy, I'm so sorry to hear that!"

Awesome! She's buyin' it! "Yeah. My... um... my guts hurt a lot. I'm so embarrassed, I didn't want to tell you... because... because I didn't want you to fall out of love with me..." Boy managed to get real tears in his eyes.

"Oh! Boy! No! Don't ever think like that! You can tell me anything!"

He took off his glasses and set them and his pocket knife down on Stump. "Will you hold these for me, Baby?" He asked in a quivering voice.

"Of course, Boy..." Stump didn't like to see Boy cry. But she was overjoyed that he was finally feeling his emotional pain. He was so sad inside. "Let it out, Boy. I'm here for you."

He pulled a handkerchief and cried into it. He wiped his eyes and blew his nose. "Oh, Stump! You're just so understanding, kind, and loving!"

He sobbed into his handkerchief for a good minute

before peering over it to make sure she was paying attention. Yep! She was. *Perfect!*

He moved his hand-kerchief away from his face and gave her the most pathetic smile he could muster.

She gently smiled back. He reached down and put a hand on Stumps strong, smooth and beautiful wood and rubbed it sensually. "You're amazing, Baby..." he said. He was obviously very moved by her loving support.

Stump felt her insides melt from his unexpected touch. Boy had a way of assuring her that everything would be okay... with just the touch of his hand. Oh, how she had missed him! Oh, how she desired to make him happy! She couldn't BELIEVE he had stayed away because of his silly embarrassment! Although she was sad he was sick, Stump was relieved to finally have some answers as to why Boy was so resistant to engaging in a healthy relationship with her.

Stump knew that physical sickness was related to unprocessed emotions in the body. Boy probably had trapped emotions in his intestines - aka dis-ease - from the terrible tummy issues he experienced when he was a kid. His family had no electricity. All he and his family had to eat was jackfruit and jalapeños and they had to light their farts on fire for heat.

Pooooooor Boy!! Poor sad, helpless, sick, embarrassed, broken, Boy! How dare she give him so much grief over using a dull knife to carve her? After everything he's been through?! She was determined to show Boy how much she loved him, and how easygoing and understanding she really was. "Boy, I'm sorry you felt like you couldn't confide in me."

"Well..." boy sniffed and wiped his eyes. "You **can** be an insufferable cunt sometimes..."

Stump was shocked. Boy must have said it without thinking. "Boy! I know you're upset, but you can't say things like that to me."

"What? What did I say?" Boy looked at Stump with weepy and confused eyes.

"You know. The c-word."

"Oh. cunt? Oh, that's not a bad word, Baby. *sniff!* It's... just means a woman who <u>C</u>an't <u>U</u>nderstand <u>N</u>ormal <u>T</u>hinking. That's all I meant, Baby. I wasn't actually calling you that.

"It's still not okay to say that to me. And I **CAN** understand normal thinking. You just aren't very fair sometimes."

"Baby, you know you don't understand logic most of the time, but... but I love you anyway." Boy brought his handkerchief to his face and softly wept as he spoke. "It's just... this irritable bowel syndrome has really got me lately... and you just don't seem very patient with me over it. And our damn president is such an ass and you don't understand the pressure I'm under just to function day to day. Please don't yell at me, Baby. I can't take it. Not today. I just can't take it!"

Wait... what? How did the conversation go from talking about the C-word to the president? Stump was so confused!

"Boy, I know you're upset. But you really hurt my feelings."

"How?"

"Because you called me that c-word. I would like an apology, Boy."

"I'm not going to apologize for something you just misinterpreted." Boy was still sniffing away, making it clear that he was the hurt one in the equation here. "I didn't do anything wrong, Baby."

Stump felt sick. She felt angry. How could she argue

with his level of denial and ignorance? Especially with him crying like this? She couldn't. She had learned many times over: arguing with Boy is just not worth it.

All was not lost, however. She had grown incredibly strong from all of the unwarranted forgiveness and love she had doled out to Boy over the years. When she looked at it this way, Boy was one of the biggest contributors to her spiritual growth. #soulmate.

Besides, this was **obviously** no time to argue with Boy! He was finally showing his vulnerable side, and she didn't want a silly squabble to ruin it. So she let his horrid comment go, accepted the apology she would never receive, and shifted her focus to the good stuff that was happening right here, right now between them. Boy was still crying; clearly a sign of a big emotional breakthrough!

Of course, Stump, being the loving earth angel who was able to forgive everything, knew she needed to do what was best for the relationship. "I'm sorry, Boy, if I've been insensitive to your needs."

"I'm just doing my best, Baby..." Boy continued to sob into his handkerchief. All I'm asking for is a toilet so I can visit you more often. I love you, Baby. I love you. I need to see you more often! My life just doesn't work without you. Can we at least agree to that much?"

Stump, too, was overwhelmed with emotion. She had no idea Boy loved her this much! Upon hearing his sweet words, she felt a joy well up inside of her and the return of her knowing that she and Boy were meant to be together. She made her decision. "Yes! Yes, my darling Boy!" She whispered lovingly. "Of course you can carve me into a toilet with your dull pocket knife from your grand-daddy, if it would mean that much to you.

"It would, Stump. It really would." Boy softly sobbed. "I've missed you so much, Stump, and if we can make this happen, I'll visit you every day." Boy was impressed with his acting ability. "I promise!"

"That will be wonderful, Boy. I'm in! Let's do this!"

"That's my girl!" Boy exclaimed. Stump felt a wave

of joy. He called her *his girl!*

Then... Boy's tears miraculously dried up. His doleful expressions morphed into cold indifference. His loving demeanor abruptly stopped. He stood up, put his glasses back on, and tucked his handkerchief back into his coat pocket.

He stepped back and sized up Stump, contemplating the best way to go about this new and exciting wood working project. He then snorted loudly, gathering the phlegm from crying into his throat, and, with dramatic flair, hocked a huge loogie right next to her. It landed on one of her roots. It felt disgusting, but Stump remained silent, secretly trying to hold on to the euphoria of knowing that she and Boy belonged together.

He knelt down next to Stump and ran an open hand across her flat wood. "Fuck, yessssss!!" Boy almost hissed. Stump shuddered. His mood was suddenly... aggressively euphoric... which made no sense to her.

Stump felt an eerie chill come over her. She suddenly felt deeply afraid, with a stark realization that this *carve-me-into-a-toilet* was actually a really bad idea. But what should she do? She already agreed to it. If she stopped him now, Boy would be so upset, and she would probably never see him again!

She began to silently chant *om* to calm her nerves: something she learned to do in her Sunday healing circle. *Oommm... oommmm... oommmm...* and forced herself to think only positive, uplifting thoughts. *This is the least I can do for our relationship. Ommmm... Boy didn't need to tell me about his irritable bowel syndrome, but he did! Oooommm... That must have been hard for him to do! Ooommmm... We love each other. This is all for the best. Ooooommmm...*

Boy scraped his knife across her flat surface. Stump winced. "Oh! Are you okay, Sweetheart?" He gently and sensually massaged the area he scraped.

"Yes, Boy. I'm okay." Stump smiled inside. He called her Sweetheart! His gentle touch felt so genuine and sweet; there was just nothing like it in the world. As her heart opened to his affections, her fear subsided. Stump realized that her hesitations about being carved into a toilet with a dull pocket-knife were RIDICULOUS!

Forgiving Boy was easy. He was a very good soul. She felt it. He gave her a deep fulfillment that no one else could ever understand. She knew her selfless, loving act today would show him, once and for all, how much she truly loved him. Her love would melt his angry shell, blast his heart open, and he would finally own up to the truth about how much he loved her. No one else could see it. But she just *knew* it.

"You are the perfect size and height for a toilet."

Hmm... not the most flattering of compliments, but it was a start. Though the scrapes from his knife were excruciating, the feel of his hands on her as he brushed away the wood chips sent blissful tingles throughout her roots. As Boy fell into a cadence of carving and smoothing, Stump was lulled into an inexplicable euphoria.

In her euphoria, she started daydreaming about her and Boy's wedding. She saw the whole day very clearly: a bonafide fairytale. She knew that, on a soul level, their wedding had already taken place. In fact, it surely existed in a parallel reality - or on some other plane, because her visualization of it was just so real! Yay!

A spring wedding would be lovely: perhaps mid April when other trees were dancing with blossoms and the wildflowers were bursting to life in brilliant, juicy colors.

However, Stump was realistic. She knew that she was a little too stout to wear taffeta, which tends to add pounds. Velvet would be too hot for a spring wedding and also had a tendency to add girth to a bride. Satin or silk in a pale ivory would bring out the natural color of her bark and accentuate her features beautifully.

She would need to start her guest list right away! Sadly, she had been out of touch with her friends and family for many years. It all started because, for some bizarre reason, Boy began telling dreadful lies about her... and they believed him. He said she was mentally ill, acting crazy, abusing him, doing drugs and drinking, neglecting responsibilities, taking his credit cards and spending his money, sleeping with other men, something about a plunger fetish... None of it made any sense. Why would he say such awful things about her? It was very perplexing. She figured he was projecting traumatic memories about his mother, who was nuts. So naturally, she forgave him.

However, she was so distressed over the loss of her friends and family that she decided to see a psychiatrist. Miraculously, during this time, Boy really stepped up; he said he wanted to do his part to heal the relationship. He accompanied her to her therapy appointments and even wanted to have some sessions by himself with the good doctor. **Obviously,** if the relationship wasn't important to Boy, he would have never done any of this. At last, Stump was hopeful!

"Miss Stump," The doctor told her solemnly one day. "All couples go through misunderstandings and trials. You seem to have a skewed perception of, and a very pronounced emotional response to normal, everyday events. I've gotten to know Boy these last few weeks.

He would never try to hurt you, or tell lies to your family." The doctor seemed deeply concerned. "In fact, if I didn't know better, I would say you are the one abusing Boy — not the other way around."

Stump burst in to gut-wrenching sobs. She had never felt so completely humiliated, invalidated, and misunderstood in all her life! "Doctor, that's not true! He does all kinds of crazy stuff! He... he hides my keys and pretends he doesn't know where they are! He deletes my favorite songs off my playlists! He steals my peanut butter! He's the one spending my money! He told terrible lies about me and turned my family against me! You've got to believe me, Doctor!"

"It's not a matter of me believing you. I'm just highly concerned. Boy also said you belong to a cult?"

"WHAT?" Stump almost shouted. "I go to a healing circle every Sunday! It gives me peace!"

"Well, from what he's described, it sounds highly suspicious."

Stump was utterly baffled. The same frustrations, and demoralizing discussions she's had with Boy over the years was now taking place with a highly trained professional! How could this even be? Unless… unless… maybe she really WAS crazy?

This notion was soon confirmed by the good doctor. "Miss Stump, you seem to be a bit paranoid and suffering from a distorted sense of reality." He then prescribed her anti-psychotics and anti-depressants and sent her to a weekly therapy group for crazy people who couldn't get a grip on life. The pills messed with her head. Three weeks later, she ended up in a psych hospital. THAT was a rough year!

During her stay at the hospital, she learned about healthy relationship boundaries. She realized that she crossed Boy's boundaries all the time! Rather than yelling or swearing to communicate with him, she needed to exercise compassion and patience. Above all, she needed to speak calmly and stop nitpicking him to death if she wanted this relationship to work.

Thus, with the help of therapy, Stump was able to

heal her life. Kinda-sorta. True, she still felt like shit about herself. She still felt even more hopeless. She still felt jumbled. But at least she was finally able to let go of the past and forgive Boy for the things that he didn't really do, and still wasn't really doing anyway... or something like that. She hoped her family and friends would one day realize that she was just going through a difficult time back then, and whatever happened between them was probably just a big mix-up.

She knew the wedding would be a glorious time of healing and love for all! Her pain was in the past now, and she would not think of it again! After all, she thought, *all we have is the present moment!*

Boy was going to make such a handsome groom! She could just see him in his dashing tuxedo, cumberbun and bow tie. *sigh!*

"Now he just needs to propose," Stump thought, "which he might even do tonight!" She imagined the look on his face when he got down on one knee. He would look deep into her bark, with tears in his beautiful eyes... so overtaken with love that he will barely be able to get the words out. "Stump, will you marry me?" "Yes, Boy, I will marry you..."

Never had Stump been more certain of anything... and never had she felt such unadulterated wholeness and peace in her heart than she did in that moment... with Boy carving her into a toilet.

How exciting! Everything she put on her vision board last year was finally coming true! The *being carved into a toilet* piece was definitely a surprise, but Almighty God works in mysterious ways!

This is the kind of love that Boy's soul needed to melt the icy walls he had built around his sad heart. If this meant Stump needed to show him how much she loved him by letting him carve her into a toilet, then by-golly! That's exactly what she would do! Willingly. Enthusiastically. Selflessly. *Carve away, my beautiful Boy! Carve away! For* **this** *is how much I love you!*

Hours passed. Boy was mostly silent as he worked. No words were needed between them. She felt his love for her. Stump heard everything he didn't say.

Her heart was overflowing in love for him. And she knew his was for her too. She could feel it. In this moment, the world was perfect. Their bodies fit together perfectly. They were made for each other. She allowed the bliss to overtake her. *sigh!*

She could never explain to anyone why she loved Boy

so much, or why she had allowed him to take her apples, her branches, her trunk... her... core. Hey! No one needed to understand. It was none of their damn business!

In all honesty, Stump knew she tolerated a lot from him. In fact, it had gotten to the point that she just no longer told people about how he was treating her, because all they ever did was judge him... or judge her in thinking she was crazy and making it all up.

No one understood their unique relationship. It's just how things needed to be until Boy was able to heal his heart, which could only happen through Stump's persistent and unconditional love.

Now, with him snuggled up to her, carving and smoothing, the waves of pleasure radiating through her roots were quintessential bliss. He was giving her his undivided attention. She knew sacrificing herself for his comfort was exactly what he needed to finally become the man she knew him to be, the man he so desperately wanted to be for her.

She could feel his breath upon her, and, if she closed her eyes and stayed very still, she could feel his heartbeat. THIS moment was a snapshot of true and perfect love... how relationships are meant to be.

Just as the sun was saying its goodnight on the horizon, Boy stood up. "Well, that's done!" His face beamed as he admired his work. "Oh! One more thing..." Boy knelt back down and started carving something into Stump's bark.

"What are you carving into my bark, Boy?" She asked with a sweet giggle. Her voice sounded hollow and without substance. Yet there was joy in her tone.

"Just hold still..." he said reassuringly.

She was excited. She figured he was carving a love poem, to memorialize their deep and abiding connection that had just been magically rekindled... due to her selfless act of kindness and understanding. Perhaps it was a quote that nuanced Stump's unconditional love and forgiveness that she consistently and generously showered upon him... a poem that spoke of how they had made it through the fires and tribulations that every healthy relationship goes through. *sigh*... *I just love him so much!*

"Excellent, excellent..." Boy said with a strange laugh. He stood, stepped back and dusted his hands. "Great! That's done!"

Stump felt a combination of relief and sadness at Boy's sudden disengagement. He was done carving... so no more pain. But also... no more of his delicious caresses from smoothing away the wood chips. Surely Boy could feel the love that was just exchanged between them? What did all this mean for their relationship? Would he keep his promise to visit her daily? Would he finally propose marriage? She was counting on her new hollowed-out look to keep him smitten. "How do I look?" She asked hesitantly.

"Like... a beautiful wooden toilet." Boy answered. Again, not the compliment she was looking for, but it was something.

"Just in time, too. I've got a train pulling into the

station that's been choo-choo-choo-ing this whole time!" Boy unbuckled his belt, pulled down his pants, and sat down. "Whew! Close call!" Pulling a newspaper from his coat pocket, he settled in for a good read.

Stump suddenly felt confused... and sick. This didn't feel right. This didn't feel good. This didn't feel like love. In fact, this situation felt really, really... crappy.

NO! She mustn't allow herself to think such terrible, selfish thoughts about her poor, emotionally broken, lost and helpless Boy. She knew he loved her. And if she could just continue to be compliant, loving, and patient, he would be able to heal from his terrible childhood and finally love her like he truly wanted to, deep inside, and underneath his gruff exterior.

Stump knew she needed to do the right thing: she sat very still, trying to be the best wooden toilet in all the land... so Boy could poop in peace. She was very grateful for being able to forgive Boy, and see the bigger picture here. She was a true lightworker!

Stump sat very still, trying to be the best wooden toilet in all the land... so Boy could poop in peace.

After 20 minutes, Boy folded up his newspaper and tossed it onto the ground. He bent down, picked up a handful of fresh wood chips, wiped his butt and threw them on top of the... steam train that lay at the bottom of Stump's newly carved hole. He stood up and pulled up his pants. "Well, that feels better!" Plucking his newspaper up from the ground, he said, "Alright, Stump! I'm outta here!"

"What??! Wait!" Stump cried. "You're leaving?! Why? I thought..."

"Yeah, I gotta get back to Fido."

"You mean... Fella...?"

"Damn it! There you go again, Stump! His name is Fido. I don't know where you got 'Fella.' What a stupid name for a dog-Fella!"

"But... Boy... I just... we just had such a beautiful time today... and I've done this nice thing here by letting you carve me..."

"Zip it, Stump! That was a lot-a work I just did for

you. My hand is cramped. Besides, you gave me a splinter in my ass. It hurts like a son of a bitch!"

Stump was baffled. She was expecting a marriage proposal, after all...

Boy turned to walk away. He felt indescribably alive. Of course, his joy would fade by the time he reached town, but his life was so depressing, and he always needed to deal with everyone else's bullshit. It was nice to come out on top for a change.

"Wait! Boy! What did you carve into my bark?"

"Oh yeah!" He beamed. "I carved a heart... "

"Aww... that's nice, Boy..."

"...with 'Stella & Boy' inside it. I forgot to tell you—I'm getting married."

Stump felt a jolt of the deepest confusion and despair imaginable. *What? How? He was marrying someone else? But... but... wait...* She felt as though she was no longer in her body. She was beside herself.

"You're getting married to another woman?!"

"Yes, I am." Boy said cheerily.

"But I... but you... but... what about us??!"

"Us? There is no us, Stump." Boy spoke scornfully and dismissively. "You know you and I are just bed buddies."

"No, Boy! Noooo! You didn't do that to me!" Stump had never felt such utter despair and humiliation.

Boy never felt such triumph and joy.

She simply couldn't hold her temper back anymore. "How could you carve another woman's name into my bark? What kind of twisted, cruel, horrible man are you??!" She burst into deep and body-wrenching sobs that echoed to the walls of the hills beyond.

"I'm the twisted, cruel, horrible one? I don't think so!" Boy said coldly. "You're the one who pushed me into another relationship because you constantly were nagging me about seeing another woman!"

Boooooyyyyy..." she wailed... "I thought... we were so happy, and you should have told me you were marrying another woman... and I let you carve me into a toilet so you would visit me every day..."

"I never said I would visit you every day. I said I could visit you every day, but you're being such a bitch that ain't ever gonna happen now!" Boy loved arguing semantics. After all, this made him one sexy motherfucker. "But you're totally acting psycho. Why would I want to visit you?"

"Boy!" Stump yelled. Through gritty tears and the deepest of angst, she spoke as forcefully as she ever had to him. "You promised to visit me every day if I let you carve me into a toilet!!!"

"No, I never said that." He turned his back to her.

Yes you did! You... you... LIAR!"

"Liar? Oh, wow. That's really mature. What's next? Are you gonna tell me my pants are on fire?"

Boy yawned and gazed at the sunset. "You see, Stump? This is why you and I would never work. You're just way, way too dramatic for me."

Whaaaaaat? Just... WHAT? How did he just put his crazy nastiness back on her? How could he yawn at a time like this? After what he just did to her?

What kind of delusional, crazy-ass monster was she dealing with here?! "What? I'm not dramatic!" Stump shrieked in vain. "Yoouu... yoouu..." Stump stammered, trying to find words to express her unfathomable pain and anger "You're...you're just a... big... fat... f... fucking... pig... ... ASSHOLE!!!!"

"God! You are one crazy bitch!" He chuckled his wicked chuckle again.

What? How could Boy laugh at her pain like this? How did he not see how hurt she was? How did he not see that she had given him EVERYTHING that ever meant anything to her – out of the goodness of her heart? How could he act so terribly unconcerned for Stump's upset and ungrateful for her stellar generosity?

How could he turn the tables on her and call **her** immature and dramatic? How could he deny that he promised to visit her every day?

Most importantly, how could he deny their deep and loving soul connection that was so evident in the incredible time they just shared today? A love that had kept him coming back to her for all these years?

Stump had no answers, only deep, all-consuming grief... and a sense of a complete obliteration of her sense of self. "Boy, don't do this to me..." Stump's desperate tone turned to one of deep mourning. "I love you, Boy. Don't leave."

"You're out of your mind!" Boy chuckled. "A minute

ago you were screaming, calling me a pig's asshole.''

"I know... but... but I didn't mean it..." Stump spoke through her sobs. "I'm just confused..."

"Oh for fuck's sake! Figure it out. And grow up!"

Stump felt an eerie darkness overtake her. Boy was walking away, taking with him everything she used to be. Her very core. Her identity. Her soul. And if that wasn't painful enough, in that blessed place where her soul once dwelled, he had dumped a giant, smelly turd.

"Oh! Hey, Stump?" Boy stopped and turned to look at her, as if he had something very important to say. "I just figured something out."

"Wwwhhat... Boy?" She could barely eek out her words. Her muggy thoughts were spinning in non-sensical jargon, in her desperate attempts to process what Boy had just done to her. Now he had something to say to her. What would it be?

Was he finally understanding how deeply hurt she

was? How wholly devastated she felt in this moment? Surely, he must care... even a little bit? Perhaps this was the moment he would confess his true feelings of love for her? The moment he would make everything right between them? Perhaps this was the moment he would apologize for being so awful to her all these years? Perhaps this was the moment he would exonerate her confusion and pain and thank her for always being there for him. Perhaps Boy was ready to profess his undying love and deep appreciation for the wonderful person Stump had been to him all their lives. Even if he were to deftly allude to any of this, it would ease her pain tremendously. Stump's very life and soul hung in the balance as she breath-lessly waited for Boy's parting words.

"I just figured out that you're full of shit." Then Boy, feeling MOST clever for his quick-witted double entendre, laughed an eerie laugh. Stump had no rebuttal. She just watched as the love of her life turned his back once more... and slowly disappeared into the sunset. She never saw him again. And she lived hollowly ever after.

The End

(Or is it?)

(She didn't know...)

(It was all up to Boy...)

(Or was it?)

... a little help?

Discussion

If you are involved in a relationship with someone who behaves and communicates like Boy – or in other ways that are equally as frustrating, you are likely experiencing narcissistic abuse.

In Shel Silverstein's The Giving Tree, the boy behaves in ways that are congruent with pathological narcissism. Please bear in mind that I use *narcissism* here as a trait – to explain his behavior – and not as a diagnosis. Narcissistic behavior is evident in any number of mental illnesses. While boy's behaviors certainly look narcissistic, it would be irresponsible of me to give Boy a psychological diagnosis of Narcissistic Personality Disorder (NPD) or any mental disorder from just a tertiary gander through The Giving Tree. The leap I make in this story – The Giving Stump, is strictly under poetic license, and for the purposes of educating my readers.

With THIS being said, this leap wasn't a hard one to make. In The Giving TREE, the boy portrays a stark lack of empathy for the pain and immeasurable loss he imposes upon his dear, lifelong *friend*. He thanklessly appropriates all things treasured by her: her apples, branches, and trunk. He shows no concern or empathy for the devastation he imposes upon her in his efforts to fulfill his own trivial whims.

In this book, The Giving Stump, I take these propensities and run with them. Throughout the story, I expanded upon the clear relationship dynamics between Stump and *the boy* in The Giving Tree, and blew them out into the open – where they can be critically and judiciously studied. I get it: there's a chance you are spinning over it. Pulling the beast into the light can invoke anxiety, disorientation, and moral outrage. But hang in there. It's about to… get worse.

In both stories, Stump (formerly known as Tree) consistently divorces herself from her truth in order to garner approval from Boy, and in futile efforts to make him happy, to keep the peace in the relationship, and, above all, make him love her. What does this costs her in terms of quality of life? Physical health? Her soul? Her personal efficacy? Her self-esteem? Her friends and familial relationships? Everything.

What She Gives vs. What He Perceives He Receives

Note the disproportionate exchange between what Stump gives Boy and what he perceives he receives; her priceless gifts almost instantly become trash. This piece is beyond spooky, and should scare the cr-apple out of you. She gives him her precious, delicious apples: he reduces them to *rotten, worm riddled sacs*. She gives him her strong, beautiful branches; he built a shanty house with them that was quickly obliterated by a storm. She gives him her life-giving and sturdy trunk; he haphazardly carves it into a boat and wrecks it. Boy denies any wrongdoing, minimizes Stump's pain and uses his rumination of his horrible experiences in ways that further abuse her.

This dynamic is exactly indicative of what happens in real life, with real humans who are subject to the real consequences of narcissistic abuse. A huge percentage of our imprisoned, homeless, and mentally-ill members of society are in their respective predicaments because they were unwitting victims of narcissistic abuse. Many were once thriving, happy, and successful individuals and positive contributors to society... who naively gave their lives and souls to the voracious appetites of narcissism. Sadly, a little bit of awareness could have saved them from such enduring and lifelong consequences.

Unconditional Love?

Stump, being the consistently kind, loving, forgiving and selfless one, with her "martyrialistic" covenant that she twists into ideals of virtue, struggles to acknowledge the truth about Boy. She does this in order to rationalize staying in this incredibly defunct relationship with him. This is a direct reflection of her level of self-love – stemming from her unprocessed emotional memory.

Boy is an extremely dangerous and mentally defective man who has no ability or intention of changing. This dynamic provides the conditions for *the perfect storm* between he and Sump. Hint: Boy is the tornado.

Who is Vulnerable to Narcissistic Abuse?

The people who are most vulnerable to narcissistic abuse are much like Stump (formerly known as Tree). They are outwardly generous, kind, fawning, sensitive people who see the good in everyone and forgive others unconditionally. They downplay and minimize their own pain in order to make other people feel better, OR to keep the peace with an otherwise volatile partner.

They are also the ones who tend to put themselves last, tend to struggle in saying *no,* and overcommit to others out or an inflated sense of guilt. Again, this all stems from a lack of self-love, and unrecognized emotional woundedness.

If you have been a victim or have closely witnessed narcissistic abuse of a loved one you will totally "get" this book. It was written for the purpose of raising your awareness and giving you words for the previously indefinable, unsolvable clusters you've found yourself– at the hands of the impossible ones.

Narcissistic abuse is deeply painful. It gouges your insides and scrambles your brain. In every way, it robs you of your joy. Once you have a good working grasp on the basics of narcissistic abuse, your true healing can begin. The next book in this series: *The Surviving Stump* (working title) will give you guidance and insight for these next steps of your journey.

Boy's Role Versus Stump's Role

It's really easy to identify Boy's abusive actions in The Giving Stump and, now that you know what to look for, The Giving Tree. What's far less discernible is Stump's role in this dysfunctional relationship. If you notice, Stump not only allows Boy's abuse, she rewards it, and, at times, even invites it. Does she like it? Of course not. But, because of his ability to psychologically manipulate her, she gives him the green light to continue.

Again, narcissism isn't so much a diagnosis, but a trait that is prevalent in many different mental health conditions. Empaths and codependents, when emotionally triggered, can also become highly defensive and toxic. People with complex post-traumatic stress response, cluster B personality disorders (e g. borderline, histrionic, antisocial) those with traumatic brain injury and even autism can display abusive behaviors. In fact, many psychology professionals assert that narcissism falls on the autistic spectrum.

I ardently **dis**agree with this notion; narcissists are deliberately vindictive, get off on the pain they inflict on others, and FEIGN ignorance to social norms in order to frustrate and harm others. They also hold deep and lasting grudges, engage in smear campaigns against anyone who dares cross them, gravely lack empathy, and have a gross entitlement mentality. They can also opportunistically morph into charming, charismatic, and socially adept people when it behooves then to do so. None of this is true for people with autism - who truly struggle in interpreting social cues and in gauging how their behaviors affect others.

In any case, be careful about labeling people as *narcissists.* At the same time, don't stick around and try to figure out, rescue, or otherwise enable an abusive person. Someone who is not a narcissist will usually want to get help and make efforts to heal their life. A narcissist will not - unless it is used as part of a manipulation or to reel back in a victim.

The Dark Triad

There are three psychological sectors of malignant mental abuse known as *The Dark Triad* – succinctly identified as follows:

Narcissism: the tendency to seek admiration, unwarranted respect, and preferential treatment from others

Psychopathy: the tendency to be extremely callous, insensitive, and ignorant of the needs or feelings of others

Machiavellianism: the tendency to coerce or manipulate others for personal gain and satisfaction

I included this information because, as you research and learn about narcissistic abuse, you will hear people refer to it often.

Personality Disorders and Narcissism:

There are ten diagnosable personality disorders in the DSM-5. Not to be confused with The Dark Triad, these ten personality disorders are categorized into three general clusters:

Cluster A (odd, eccentric types: paranoid, schizoid, schizotypal)

Cluster B (dramatic, emotional, erratic types, and most abusive)

Cluster C (anxious, fearful types: avoidant, dependent, O.C.D.)

Although all personality disorders can lead to experiences of narcissistic abuse, Cluster B personality disorders are recognized as the group that lead to purposeful, manipulative abuse through exploitation of a victim's own unrecognized woundedness / weaknesses. Note that traits can cross over into any of the other. Often, narcissists present as "personality disorder Not Otherwise Specified (N.O.S.). This is due to their constant *shapeshifting* in order to exploit different victims, in different ways.

Focus on Cluster B:

Antisocial: (I will purposely hurt you and laugh in your face while I do it – and secretly or overtly delight in your resulting pain.)

Histrionic: (I'm gorgeous, brilliant, sexy… and you're not… and YOU BETTER NOT FUCKING PISS ME OFF, YOU

STUPID SLUT! Oh- hey! I like your shoes.)

Narcissistic: (I'm entitled to anything good that you have. I'll do whatever I can to get it. And if you cross me, you'll be sorry!)

Borderline: (I love you! I hate you! I need you! Please stay! Get away from me!) Note: a narcissist can, like he did with Stump, coerce her into behaving in ways consistent with Borderline Personality Disorder. However, it's much more likely that Stump is suffering from what is now being referred to by narcissism experts as *Complex Post Traumatic Stress Response.*

For simplicity, all resulting manipulation and abuse from Cluster B personality disorders are thrown under the *narcissism* umbrella. For the purposes of this book, I refer to all of it as narcissism and narcissistic abuse – again, to describe the traits and behaviors – not to dole out a conclusive diagnosis.

Regardless, the reality is that a victim is often the one pegged as the narcissist in the relationship, and the true narcissist positions himself as the victim.

Enough of this psychobabble. On to definitions!

Definitions

Narcissist: a conceited, manipulative person (sometimes he can be extremely passive who works to either overtly or covertly control you. A narcissist typically demands that you forgo personal beliefs, comforts, plans, and other essentials in order to serve him as a superior being. A narcissist will exploit your trust, possessions, money, children, manipulate your kindness (which they view as weakness) purposely scramble your brain, devalue you and corrupt your personal peace - all for his own personal gain. Most of the time, watching you suffer, grovel, cry, or rebel is all the reward a narcissist needs. They "feed" on the suffering of other people.

Narcissistic Relationship: A relationship with demonstrated narcissistic behaviors, in which one person is the abuser, and the other is the victim. It's important to know that narcissism has many "flavors" and can be extremely hard to detect. Often, the victim is the one who looks guilty of being the abuser because she is so frustrated and worn out.

Manipulation: Manipulation is purposeful, skillful influence imposed upon another person or group of people for selfish gain. Manipulation tactics vary. Some narcissists manipulate by demonstrating a pervasive sense of helplessness, thus garnering inordinate time and attention from their victims. Others play dumb and try to convince the victim that they didn't mean any harm by their obviously hurtful words or behaviors. Still others give terrible, even insulting gifts – then feign offense when their victim isn't thrilled. For example, a narcissistic man might buy his wife a wilted bouquet of flowers, a pair of slippers that are far too small for her (larger) feet, or a cheap coffee mug with a picture of a sexy woman in a bikini on it with the inscription, "You're hot like the coffee in this mug!" When she looks at him with annoyance, he will then say, "Why are you so annoyed? I'm giving you a compliment by giving you this mug!" followed by, "Geesh! I try to do something nice for you, and this is what I get?!" He hammers it home. *Guilt! Guilt! Guilt! Guilt! Confusion! Guilt!* until she caves and apologizes to him, and finally thanks him for the stupid mug – if, for no other reason than to keep the peace.

One of the BEST worst gifts I've ever heard of is this: for their anniversary, a woman's narcissistic husband gave her a cast iron bronzed replica of his penis. She was mortified. But, not understanding narcissism at the time, and concerned she might hurt his feelings, she laughed it off and chalked it up to a *moment of stupid* on his part. She quickly hid the dreadful doorknob on a top shelf in their garage, where it would be safe from the inquisitive eyes of their two small children. He became angry, plucked it off the shelf, and INSISTED that it stay on the mantel in their living room. The ensuing battle was bitter and long – with him relentlessly accusing her of being a rude, spoiled, high maintenance wife who was horribly unappreciative of his amazing and heartfelt gift that any other woman in the world would have been THRILLED to receive. *(Ch-yahh! Totally! The pretentious bitch!)*

Beware that narcissism shows up not just in romantic relationships, but friendships, families, neighbors, teachers, coworkers and, especially supervisors. Since narcissists lack empathy, they have NO trouble staying cool and collected while setting up their peers to look like incompetent, emotional idiots. Clusters of narcs appear in social circles, schools, work environments, churches, and governing boards where many egos can compete for a chance to and puff up their respective chests and intimidate others into irrational submission.

Smear Campaign: A smear campaign is a purposeful, vengeful, defamation of your name, reputation and character. The narcissist will create **false narratives** in order to make you look like a devious, selfish, inept person which, ironically, is an exact projection of who he truly is. Motivations for smear campaigns vary. Sometimes it's because you've figured out that something is wrong with him. Perhaps you don't worship him like you're supposed to, or concede to him as the all-knowing authority on (any given subject). He may be jealous of your looks, charisma, popularity, intelligence, or spiritual light (beautiful, spiritual, and intelligent people beware! You are especially delicious targets for narcs.) Some narcs launch smear campaigns so they can exploit or appropriate something you have (like a lover, money, property, pets, children etc...). Many times, smear campaigns are launched simply because you're happy and confident or have something that makes a narc feel inferior. In his mind, you are hurting him on purpose, and, therefore, deserve to suffer. He decides to ravage your reputation and your life, and will relish your struggle and fall. Don't try to understand it; narcissism, as a whole, baffles normal, rational people.

Projection: Because of the fact that his sense-of-self is missing, self-reflection is impossible for the narcissist. He gets his sense-of-self solely from the feedback of others. This also means he will never own up to his mistakes (except when trying to hoover a victim). Rather, he projects his mistakes, along with his own sense of ineptness, faults, selfishness, and other deficits onto those around him. Blame is the name of the game. Shockingly, he believes his own projections, and can, therefore, be most convincing to others. While he's at it, he'll take credit for her accomplishments and hard work. This is why narcissists are also referred to as pathological liars.

Sense-of-Self: Having a sense of self means having an inherent understanding that one exists separately from the world, and not as an extension of it or others. Children and teens naturally go through a (crucial) individuation process in order to develop their own sense-of-self - as evident by the "terrible twos" and teenage rebellion. If these processes are thwarted by overbearing parents, siblings, society, bullies, church authorities, or other adults, the child could fail to individuate, and narcissism or co-dependency could result. An external view of himself becomes the framework of his or her existence.

Both the narcissist and codependent suffer from a damaged sense-of-self. For the narcissist, the sense-of-self is completely non-existent, which, while very sad, is what makes him so dangerous. The sense-of-self is essentially how a person sees (and "senses") himself in relation to the world. A healthy person has an intrinsic sense-of-self that coexists within a larger environment and the world. A person who lacks a sense of self, on the other hand, is dependent upon his life circumstances and other people to show him who he is. This is why a narcissist gets so hostile with those who dismiss or insult him.

Note that both the narcissist and codependent struggle to own their sense of self. Here's the difference: the codependent will seek therapy, forgiveness, and other means to try to fix her life and *figure it out*; the narcissist takes no ownership of his personal problems, and will constantly blame others for them.

Codependent: A person who is at risk for narcissistic abuse; a codependent person is happy only if her partner is happy with her. She's scared when her partner is angry, she feels good about herself if her partner expresses love or gratitude towards her, etc... Stump clearly suffers from codependency... which is what makes her so vulnerable to Boy's continual abuse.

Note that codependent people evolve as highly empathic and intuitive people; this is an adaptive survival response for navigating a hostile world. This is why codependents are often referred to as empaths. (It's also why so many broken people end up as psychics – so beware!) Some good news here is, once a codependent heals and transforms her own woundedness and regains her sense of self, her empathy remains and becomes highly refined and her intuition skyrockets.

False Self: Narcissists are devoid of their true self. In its place, they assert their false self. The false self is exactly what it purports: a falsely constructed version of who a person truly is. In general, this refers to the sense of existing within one's own being, and separate from others. Often (but not always) the false self is confident, manipulative, and cunning, constantly seeking ways to exploit others for control and feeding their sense of superiority. Codependents also struggle with a false self but they haven't lost their true selves entirely. Codependents are also capable of feeling guilt, empathy and healing. Generally, a true narcissist is not - though some narcissists are riddled with guilt for their behaviors. Instead of apologizing, they *make up for it* by gift giving, being especially loving, or extending random acts of kindness toward the victim. This is sometimes part of hovering, and all plays into the mastermind of control the narc exerts over his victim.

Narcissistic Supply: Metaphysically speaking, narcissistic supply is a victim's life force energy. It's a person's chutzpah, drive, joy, soul... and a most delicious nom-nom to the narcissist's empty soul. A narcissist can garner narcissistic supply through any number of means, with the goal being to deregulate a victim's thoughts, beliefs, personal peace, confidence, freedom, reputation, relationships, health, or financial solvency.

A narcissist feels entitled to destroy other people's lives in order to make himself feel better, because he believes he is better than everyone in some way. (He's better looking, better with money, in better health, is more intelligent, is stronger or physically more agile than others, etc...) Again, don't try to understand it - just recognize that there is a virus in his mental hardware, and you need to protect yourself by staying as far away from him as possible. Just like you can't protect yourself from a cold or the flu by freaking out and yelling at an infected person, you can't protect yourself from narcissism by freaking out or yelling at him either. He will use your emotional outburst as a direct line into your psyche and flood you with his infection.

There is some hope though: like those with healthy immune systems, you can become inoculated from the narc virus. Your first steps are educating yourself and raising yourself awareness - which is exactly what this book is about. Woot!

False Narrative: False narratives are lies told by the narcissist that come out of absolutely nowhere. The accusations, rumors, and stories are complete fiction, borne and in the mind of the narcissist for the *soul* purpose of demoralizing his target. False narratives are *custom designed* to trigger shame in his target – which is easily accomplished because the narcissist constructs false narratives from his targets' identified *emotional weak spots*. Creating false narratives makes no sense to us sane, rational and honest folks who value the truth, cooperation, and respectful relationships. Remember that the narcissist isn't after truth, respect or cooperation; he is after narcissistic supply, which can only be garnered by triggering emotional reactions in others. We see false narratives often in professional circles as narcissists seek to only cover their own respective asses, but to climb the corporate ladders to success and power. Since false narratives can (understandably) trigger moral outrage victims, by the time the lies reach the "higher ups" in any given company, everyone is just talking about the victim's reaction, not the actual lies that triggered such reactions. Therefore, if you find you're ever the target of a false narrative, the best way to deal with it is to do whatever you can to calm your reactive anger to it. EFT can be HUGELY helpful in this regard, as EFT literally quells the stress response in the body. If you don't emotionally "resonate" with the narc's false narrative, chances are it won't have the impact he seeks, and you will have a much easier time debunking it. Speak the truth as SOON as you hear the rumblings, and speak it calmly and widely. Address it right away. Tread lightly, but do address it. A word of caution: don't get caught up with trying to defend yourself, for this is also a way for the narc to garner supply from you. *(Big thanks to Jerry Graves for his excellent discussion on this topic: Dealing with Narcissist's False Narratives at Work: September 24, 2018, YouTube)*

Entitlement: The narcissist holds a grandiose belief that he is more important, superior, or brilliantly unique than other people. This means, in his mind, that he should receive special treatment, privileges, attention, and other resources that are not afforded to commoners. E.g.: he should not need to wait in line like everyone else, he should receive special pricing (or free admission) to an event, he should be able to take the apples, branches, and trunk of his best friend, Tree, without so much as a thank you, and will believe with every ounce of his being that the tree "owes" him these things and should be thanking him for his time and attention. A sense of entitlement is what prompts a narcissist to exploit others for personal gain.

Triangulation: An abuser will often intentionally engage a third party (real or imagined) such as another person, group, or entity (e.g.: a governing board) into the relationship in order to further abuse a victim. This is called triangulation. He successfully manipulates this third party into believing terrible things about the victim that aren't true. The purpose of triangulation is to "spread the crazy" and turn the third party into a flying monkey to help carry out his narcissistic abuse against the victim. This causes grave distress for the victim who usually ends up clinging to the narcissist and trying to explain herself and her innocence.

Especially, narcissists will use gossip, outright lies, and their own perverse projections to turn team others against his victim. Since the narcissist is extremely skilled at identifying other people's wounds and weakness, all he needs to do is to exploit identified wounds or weakness, and then blame the triangulated party.

For example, a narcissist might tell a woman who is worried about how she looks in a swim suit, "I can't believe Kim said you have cellulite. I think you look great. She's not a very good friend." Of course, Kim never said her friend had cellulite, but such a statement will emotionally blind the victim and she will become hurt or angry with Kim for saying such a thing. When people are emotional, they are extremely vulnerable to suggestion. Therefore, with his victim upset, the narcissist will easily convince the woman she should stop being friends with Kim altogether, because she (Kim) is obviously two-faced. This is one of the ways that narcissists isolate victims from friends, relatives, neighbors, and colleagues. Isolation is a key part of narcissistic abuse because it gets rid of people who might raise eyebrows to the narc's questionable behaviors.

Ghosting: Sometimes the narcissist will just disappear from the relationship without explanation, without warning, without texting, calling, or communicating in any way. This sudden "ignoring" of the victim is completely intentional. It usually happens after an intense period of intimacy and affection. It seems to come out of nowhere; its purpose is to utterly baffle and confuse a victim and send her into an all-consuming anxiety in trying to figure out what she did wrong. Her anxiety feeds the narcissist's false ego – confirming that he, indeed, is extremely important, desirable, etc… or she wouldn't be so upset about him leaving. Thus, the process of ghosting gives him huge amounts of narcissistic supply. We only see ghosting in The Giving Stump in retrospect, when discussing Boy's habit of staying away from Stump for long periods of time, with absolutely no communication and no explanation. His walking away at the end of the story is more of a *discard* than ghosting.

Stonewalling: Stonewalling is different from ghosting; it usually happens while still in the physical presence of the victim. It denotes a complete "shut down" and refusal to communicate, usually over an extremely important subject. Stonewalling is a form of emotional abandonment in a relationship. For example, if a victim confronts her husband with evidence that he's having an affair, rather than defend himself or allay his wife's fears, he will just stonewall her. He'll just shut down and refuse to talk about it – or anything. Stonewalling is a way to punish her for questioning him. It is especially useful to manipulate and garner control over a victim who is desperately seeking approval, attention, and connection from her partner.

Love-Bombing: over-the-top compliments, expressions of love and affection, gifts, admiration, attention, compassion, and devotion from the narcissist. Love bombing normally happens in the beginning of a relationship or can be used in hoovering. It garners a victim's trust and secures emotional attachment to the narcissist. Once she is hooked, the devaluation stage begins.

Trauma Bonding: A powerful psychological bond that stems from survival instincts. Trauma bonding arises from the experience of intense pain (physical or emotional) coupled with intense pleasure. The human brain sees a person who delivers pain and pleasure as very important, and biological, hormonal, and neurological processes all work overtime to bond to such an individual.

[5]**Flying Monkey:** Also referred to as *minions,* Flying monkeys

are people who orbit around and fawn after the approval and favor of a bully or narcissist. In general, they behave this way in efforts to stay safe and promote their own well-being. Flying monkeys are very common in abusive work environments and

---

[5] *Flying monkey picture courtesy of https://commons.wikimedia.org/wiki/File:Wizard04.jpg*

abusive homes; terrified workers / siblings turn against each other in order to garner the favor of the abusive supervisor / parent. Most of the time, flying monkeys know exactly what they are doing, realize it is wrong, and make a conscious decision to do it anyway. In some cases, however, they are unknowingly manipulated by the narcissist and pitted against a target. Flying monkeys will support and defend the narcissist as they are too psychologically weak or opportunistic, to take a stand for what's *right*. People with fragile self-esteems are often highly susceptible to being a flying monkey.

Splitting: Splitting is a psychological mechanism that splits reality by dividing all people (including the self) into *all bad* or *all good* extremes. There are no shades of gray. Reality is black or white, right or wrong. People are powerful or powerless and reduced to either winners or losers. As narcissism is a common trait in adolescence, we often see this type of extreme criticism and judgment in teens, which is why cliques and groups are so delineated in junior high and high schools.

Denial: a cowardly abuse tactic of blatant lying to protect one's self, confuse a victim, or brainwash a victim into believing an explicit or implicit lie. To the unaware, denial is absolutely crazy-making because the playing field of a fair discussion and argument is effectually non-existent. (How can you argue with a delusion that's fiercely protected as absolute truth in the mind of the deviant? You can't.) The most malevolent narcissists routinely use denial as a way to control, upset, and purposefully destroy their victims. Because of the sheer magnitude of manipulations that must be waded through in order in attempts to get to the truth, most empaths (victims / codependents- who are perpetually fawning to please the abuser anyway) will resolve to "let it go" because it's "not worth the trouble." Think of the song "It Wasn't Me" by Shaggy to understand how perverse and rudimentary denial is for the narcissist. In the face of blatant, irrefutable evidence, he will simply keep repeating, "It wasn't me," or "I didn't do it."We see this perverse denial all the time with serial killers and rapists. Harvey Weinstein is a perfect example!

Devaluing: The stage of the narcissistic relationship that comes after a victim is "hooked" on an abuser. The narcissist, without warning, "flips the switch" from his kind, loving, generous, and attentive side, to a cold, callous, cruel, and insulting side. When in the devaluing phase, the narcissist displays a stark lack of empathy, lack of gratitude, lack of appreciation for the victim. Devaluing the victim is meant to garner control by disorienting and upsetting her into a frenzy of trying to get back to their previously wonderful, fairytale-like relationship.

Projection: occurs when someone blames another person for his own beliefs, behaviors, or attitudes. Example: a cheating boyfriend will vehemently accuse his girlfriend of cheating on him. Often, he has no idea he's projecting his own guilt outwardly. Interesting sidebar: projection is the basis of psychological tests such as the Rorschach (ink-blot) test, or even cloud-watching. If you are cloud watching with your romantic partner and he says he sees a pole dancer spanking a pony with his grandma's girdle, beware! And run!

Narcissistic Rage: An angry fit thrown by a narcissist order to shock another into submission, elicit fear, or otherwise garner control over a victim or group of victims. Narc rages most often happen in response to someone catching them in a lie or questioning their authority or other quality that is part of their fake mask of superiority. A raging narcissist is very dangerous. In at least some cases, the narcissist believes he is perfectly justified in his anger.

Hoovering: Coined from the famous vacuum cleaner company, a narcissist will do and say whatever he can in order to suck a disengaged / disinterested victim back into his life so he can continue abusing her. Hoovering can be something as simple as putting a *like* on a victim's social media post or as elaborate as orchestrating a flash mob marriage proposal. Many times, hoovering involves apologies, gifts and flattery and is generally tailored to whatever is most important to the victim.

Hypervigilance: A tendency for a victim to keep a nervous, watchful "eye" on the external environment. The narcissistic "rules" are constantly changing, and the victim never knows what will upset him. Hyper-startle response (jumping at loud noises) etc... indicates that a victim has subconsciously adapted hypervigilance in efforts to survive the narcissistic environment.

Cognitive Dissonance: (CogDis): Holding a specific belief or truth and simultaneously taking action against it. For example, if you hold the belief that a romantic partner should be caring, respectful and kind, and your romantic partner is disrespectful, hurtful, and mean, you will experience cognitive dissonance. Cognitive dissonance is resolved by:

1) changing your belief

2) changing your action

3) changing your perception of the action (*rationalization*)

Efforts to fill the CogDis gap vary. Example of such efforts might be fawning after an abuser, overanalyzing his actions or inactions, or even making a phone call to your psychic. Note: if the dissonance cannot be resolved, you will experience mental stress that can lead to clinical depression, anxiety, even a mental breakdown. Narcissist's purposely instigate CogDis and get off on seeing how far a victim will go before she *snaps*. This gives them huge doses of narcissistic supply.

Gaslighting: A form of mental manipulation used to make a victim question herself, her reality, her memory, or her sanity. Coined from the famous 1938 play by Patrick Hamilton, Gaslight, and its later 1940 and 1944 movie renditions, a covertly abusive husband psychologically tortures his wife by (among other devious acts) secretly dimming the home's gas lamps. Today, an abuser may hide his girlfriend's phone, wallet, purse or other object - then claim to have no idea where it is when she starts frantically looking for it. An abuser can get creatively elaborate in his efforts to gaslight a victim as this technique affords him huge doses of narcissistic supply.

Word Salad: *Just like driving a car you don't always need to put monkey in trunks. It goes better if mean the sun shines in your shoes for dancing one.* This sentence is an example of word salad in the traditional clinical sense; it sounds like English (or whatever one's native language is) but doesn't actually make sense. Word salad is typical in schizo disorders, brain disorders, and dementia – and, in such cases, is not intentional. Narcissists, however, use word salad deliberately, to confuse and control their victims. In narcissism, word salad sometimes shows up as circular conversations that just don't go anywhere. You can, in a way, think of word salad as a "catch all" manipulation tactic for any narc communication that create frustration, guilt, shame, fear, confusion, or cognitive dissonance in a victim.

Secondary Abuse: Secondary abuse occurs when the victim seeks protection, help, or guidance from family members or friends; these family members and friends then deny the victim's view point, telling her she's not taking responsibility, is just feeling sorry for herself, and/or refusing to see the real problem in her relationship correctly. In other words, the family member or friend will side with the narcissist and refuse to listen to the victim, even becoming angry when the victim continues to try to explain herself. Usually secondary abuse occurs because the narcissist has already triangulated the family member/friend and told his twisted and tainted version of the story. All of this causes the victim to question her objective reality and the reality of the abusive situation, and thus prompts deep despair.

Tertiary Abuse: Even worse than secondary abuse is tertiary abuse. This is when unaware therapists or other mental health / medical professionals side with the narcissist while treating the victim. This adds a whole new level of victory to the narcissistic abuse... and damage and devastation to the victim.

Blame Shifting: A cleverly instigated ploy used to shift the focus of any argument OFF of the abuser and deflect it ONTO the victim. One of many examples in the story of blame shifting occurs when Boy told Stump about wrecking the boat – which was made out of Stump's trunk. When she gets upset and calls him out, he quickly blames her for growing bad, porous wood. She then catches him in a lie: porous wood wouldn't sink. He asserts that she "can't let anything go!" and retorts, "You wanna shut your pie hole and stop calling me a liar?" Stump is then left defending herself; the blame has been successfully shifted off of Boy and onto her. Blame shifting is a big part of the victim never having any resolution to any argument with a narcissist.

<end definition list>

This list is by no means exhaustive. I could write an entire encyclopedia on narcissistic abuse-and still not fully conceptualize this complex and dangerous phenomenon... a phenomenon that silently plagues the moral fiber of humanity. However, this definition list gives you a working knowledge of narcissism to help you understand how you may have been affected in your life by it. It is more than enough to help you as you work to regain your sense of self and sovereignty.

Teasing Apart the Crazy

Warning: this part gets a little intense. What I've done is broken the story into small pieces and discussed each piece in terms of narcissistic abuse. This process can teach you to recognize and conceptualize the sometimes extremely subtle, confusing maneuvers of narcissistic abuse (it's likely that you missed at least half of them in the story). Since this section could be emotionally triggering for you, as was writing it for me, just go at your own pace. Perhaps read one page or one section a day. Remember, too, whatever emotionally surfaces for you is coming up for your awareness. See your therapist as needed and definitely up your self-care. Avoid other stressors if you can. Okay? Let's go!

The Giving Stump

Even the title of this book was chosen with great thought. What can a stump give? Is it not obvious she has already given too much?

"You are a very hard stump," the boy said scornfully. He shifted his seat, trying to get comfortable.

Our story begins with Boy delivering a shaming statement over an unchangeable aspect of Stump's physical makeup. His insult wasn't so much in his words, but in his shifting in his seat, trying to get comfortable – while telling her, "You are a very hard stump." Well golly - thank you, Captain Obvious! She's a tree stump, not an easy chair. If anyone were to actually point out this insensitivity to Boy, he would feign ignorance and say, "What's the big deal? I just made an innocent comment. Geesh! Lighten up!" (Minimizing, denial.)

Stump felt her roots shiver with a familiar disparity. She thought of every way possible to make herself softer, but there is only so much **soft** that can be bamboozled out of oneself when you are a tree stump.

Shame and a sense of disparity are common reactions to the narcissist's passive-insults and lurid expectations. The disparity causes the victim to panic, trying to figure out how to "close the gap" between what or whom she is (a hard stump) and what the narcissist desires (a soft place to sit).

Stump had no branches and, therefore, no leaves to pillow his bony, old butt, while he sat on her... contemplating his miserable and cluster-fucked life.

Underneath their manipulative, rude, and toxic personalities, narcissists are miserable, lonely, and empty with perpetually "cluster-fucked" lives.

She tried to think of happy things to talk about in order to distract him from his discomfort.

Judging from her reactionary efforts to comfort and appease Boy, it is very likely that Stump was reared in an emotionally and /or physically unsafe home environment with at least one irrational, reactive, controlling, very depressed parent or other significant adult figure. In such a home environment, a child learns to distract, entertain, comfort, and nurture the volatile parent in order to garner love and approval and to get her physical and emotional needs met. This child will grow into an adult who feels panicky or fearful if any adult around her becomes angry or disapproving. She will fall into these same fawning / pleasing patterns as an adult.

"Boy, do you remember when I let you pick my apples so you could sell them? Did that make you happy?""

"Your apples?!" Boy curled his lip in disgust. "Good God, no, Stump! You know I didn't make a cent off those rotten, worm- riddled sacs."

Narcissists exploit their victims' goodness and gifts. Then, later, insult those same gifts, claiming that their benefits were weak, non-existent, or even detrimental. Or, as we soon see, he may claim that he did her a favor by taking the gift from her.

Stump's heart dropped and thumped heavily. She was dumbfounded. What was Boy saying about her precious and perfect apples? They were rotten? Worm riddled? Preposterous! "Um... Boy? Uh... you're mistaken. My apples were neither rotten nor worm- riddled." she spoke gently but firmly, just like she had been taught in her self-assertiveness training.

Speaking up and speaking the truth is never easy for a codependent. This is because she is dependent upon the other person's mood and feedback to feel safe, loveable, and accepted. If she upsets him, she stands to suffer intense emotional consequences. This is a result of needing to acquiesce to a tyrannical parent or other adult figure during childhood and/or teenage-hood.

"They most certainly were!" Boy barked back.

Boy's statements are false and provide a double-barreled blast to Stump: 1) grief over the loss of her dear apples, and 2) shame for her gifts not being valued. Something extremely dear to her that she gave up / sacrificed for him is unappreciated, scorned, viewed as a burden. This is a very cruel (though common) form of mental abuse used by narcissists and is almost never obvious to outsiders.

Stump jumped at Boy's abrupt comeback. Her heart thumped. She was stumped. Perhaps Boy was just confused.

Victims almost never understand or believe that the abuser is actually abusing her – or that he is purposefully delivering a false account in order to elicit narcissistic supply. Believing a narcissist is "just confused" or somehow misunderstands the issue, or is just not remembering the right event, or remembering the event correctly - all of the mental "hoops" a victim's brain jumps through in efforts to make sense of the narcissist's hurtful claims is all very common for the victim. I call this "chasing the false ghouls." Any discussion, arguing, or contra-talk is banter that the narcissist will enjoy immensely, which will allow him to garner plenty of narcissistic supply from her. Also, note that he will never, ever, EVER concede - even if she presents him with ample evidence that he's incorrect, and she is right. He sees any disagreement from a victim as a green light to metaphorically obliterate her resolve.

She knew her apples were wonderful and delicious. She wouldn't have given them to him if they weren't.

Boy's goal is to get Stump to divorce her own knowing that her apples were of excellent quality – or at the very least, get her to shut up about the truth. He does this because it makes him feel almost God-like and powerful – to be able to wield another person's reality. Be aware: this type of purposefully manipulative behavior is indicative of grave mental pathology.

Her baby apples were very dear to her. She had given them to Boy out of the goodness of her heart so he would know how much she loved him. For these many years, the only thing that gave her comfort over the loss of her beautiful apples was the knowing that Boy had made money selling them - to hungry people who were nourished by their deliciousness.

Victims often comfort themselves with renditions of reality that serve to remind them of their generosity and virtue. This is because the narcissist rarely, if ever shows up for the victim in this way… in a way that a normal, healthy person would show up in a relationship.

"You should be grateful I took those appalling apples off your hands," he said flatly.

A narcissist turns his abusive or exploitative action into a "favor" he did for the victim.

"They shouldn't even be called apples. They should be called appalls." Boy gave a snarky laugh. "Get it? Because they were so appaaaalllling?" Boy belly-laughed and snorted.

Making jokes at the victim's expense is commonplace for narcs.

Stump didn't answer him for holding back her tears. She hoped Boy wouldn't notice how upset she was; that never went well.

A victim knows that showing her emotions makes her vulnerable to criticism from an abusive partner. Therefore, she works hard to stay stoic

and unemotional in his presence. Purposely upsetting another person —
especially a kind and gentle person, is baffling to those of us who are not
narcissistic. We don't want to believe that other people are capable of
this behavior. But, if you've lived through abuse like this, you are likely
nodding in understanding and recognizing these patterns.

"HellooOOOO?" Boy jeered. "What? You're not going

to answer me or laugh at my jokes now? How rude!"

A narc will rarely pass up an opportunity to twist the knife. He will beat
a joke to death if it means he is able to continue upsetting his victim. He
will then find some way to fault her for her reaction (upset) – which is
very often twisted into a projection of his own behavior. In this example,
"How rude!" is a purposeful knife twist from Boy that projects his own
rudeness. What do you think he would say to Stump if she came back
with, "You're the one who is being rude by calling my apples appalls!"
Well, it would be something to the effect of, "Oh, lighten up! What?
You can't take a joke?" There is this constant double standard that the
narc wields as a metaphorical tool of mass destruction.

She had grown her apples from tiny buds. She
nourished and doted on them for an entire season.
She raised them to be upstanding, healthy apples.
When Boy picked them, she was giving him a very
dear piece of herself.

*Here we see Stump's self-assurance that she **isn't crazy**.*

Strangely, the mere thought of her apples being rotten
and wormy brought up feelings of deep shame This
made defending her apples positively gut-wrenching!

Narcissists are masters at sniffing out and exploiting subconscious emotional wounds in their victims. Boy's insulting Stump's apples here is intentional; he knows it will elicit shame for her. This shame makes it very easy to manipulate her and elicit narcissistic supply. This is also why Stump can simultaneously know her apples are very high quality and react to his accusations as if they weren't.

Stump desperately wanted to correct Boy's very faulty memory of her apples. "Boy," her voice quivered, "many people used to tell me my apples were extremely delicious. I don't understand why you would say..."

*The fact that a narcissist is being purposely hurtful by making blatantly false statements usually doesn't occur to the victim. Instead, she concludes that he is misinterpreting the situation or experiencing faulty memory. Sadly, instead of just chalking up his incongruent behavior to **his** mental illness, she spins in her own shame and frustration, trying to make sense of it... and at the same time, tries to get him to see reality.*

"You know those people were all lying to you," Boy interrupted her. "They felt sorry for you because, obviously, you're a bit pathetic. You know I always tell you the truth, even if it hurts."

*Obviously, Boy lied to Stump about her apples being rotten and wormy. This lie is designed to elicit predictable shame in Stump – as she is much easier to manipulate while in a shame-induced emotional state. To back this lie, he told another lie and pushed it onto a third party ("**those people** were all lying to you.") He then proclaimed that he "always tells the truth, even if it hurts." Of course, this statement, itself, is complete horseshit. The only shred of TRUTH in his statement is IT HURTS."*

Narcissists make facts out of lies for the purpose of frustrating and upsetting victims. Narcissists "layer" the lies, so even if the victim busies herself by defending one, there are seven more unaccounted lies in the narc's verbal "pod" that will remain unaccounted for. Note, too, that each lie supports the other, creating an impossible net of unsolvable frustration for the victim:

1) *"I didn't make a cent..." LIE! Yes he did.*

2) *"...off those rotten..." LIE! They weren't rotten.*

3) *"...worm-riddled sacks" LIE! They didn't have worms.*

4) *"Those people were all lying to you. " LIE! Boy is the one lying.*

5) *"They felt sorry for you." LIE! This statement is meant to verify his lie that they felt sorry for her.*

6) *"Obviously, you're a bit pathetic." LIE! There's nothing pathetic about Stump... except her relationship choices.*

7) *"I always tell you the truth..." LIE! Boy never tells her the truth. His whole goal in this relationship is to mine Stump for her precious life force energy - which is collected through scrambling reality, shoving it down her throat, and getting her to divorce her truth.*

8) *"...even if it hurts." LIE! Boy suggests here that he's virtuous and honest. Nothing about Boy is honest. Nothing about this relationship is fair. The ONLY truth in Boy's statement is "it hurts."*

What Boy didn't tell Stump is this: he actually made a killing off her apples. It just wasn't enough money to pay off his massive gambling debts. So technically, he wasn't lying. Plus, he only gambled because Stump was such an annoying nag. He needed to distract himself from her infernal yammering. Therefore, obviously, his debt was all her fault.

Because Boy didn't make enough money from Stump's apples to pay his gambling debt (which he never mentioned as his reason for needing money in the first place), it caused him to experience stress. Because of his false self, he is virtually unable to take any responsibility for his actions that have caused (said) stress. The responsibility for his stress is, "projected" onto the nearest target. His rationalization of "technically, he wasn't lying" makes PERFECT sense to Boy's false self. Stump has willingly been the dumping ground for Boy's projections for many years. Keep in mind, readers, that this pathological lying and rationalization makes perfect sense to Boy. He doesn't even realize that he's lying. He does NOT see it as dishonest or harmful by any stretch.

Stump didn't speak for several minutes. She was twisted in angst and trying to make sense of Boy's ludicrous account of her beloved apples. How on earth could he remember her decadent and delicious apples as being rotten and wormy? And was she REALLY pathetic? Were all those people REALLY lying to her? None of this made any sense! But Boy... he was her soulmate. He would never lie to her...

Here we see Stump in a moment of cognitive dissonance. This is why she is "twisted with angst." Stump knows her apples were excellent, yet she doesn't want to disagree with Boy or cause "tension" in the relationship. Further, she doesn't want to face the reality that Boy is capable of lying.

In the next section, observe how Stump divorces her own truth about her apples in order to keep the peace and appease Boy. This is very important, because this is the very process – divorcing her own truth – that erodes her self-esteem and makes her a slave to Boy's mental illness.

Stump finally decided to be the bigger person and just let it go... and avoid any further argument. She knew that the best approach to this silly misunderstanding was unconditional love and forgiveness.

Unconditional love and forgiveness are popular notions with most religious and spiritual groups. However, when it comes to dealing with narcissists, this can be a psychologically dangerous approach. "Unconditional forgiveness" usually translates into "no accountability" for the narcissist, and he is permitted to continue his abusive actions with virtually no consequence. In fact, he is rewarded with his victim's compliance and, like Dracula, takes it upon himself to suck her life force dry. He never needs to look within himself – something we only do when we are in pain. He doesn't even have a chance to heal or transform his pathology - which are stemming from childhood wounds that are causing his narcissism in the first place. A missed opportunity for the narcissist - one that will enable and reward his pathological tendencies - and one that is absolutely deadly for the victim.

Now, does this mean a victim should take it upon herself to exact revenge? No, of course not. We will discuss the role of forgiveness later in the book in more detail. For now, know that forgiveness and enabling are two different things!

She was in love with Boy! They needed each other.

Stump's "love" for Boy is actually an emotional neediness that springs from her deep childhood woundedness. Pay attention here: this disparity is indicative of traumatic emotional memory that is seeking to be healed, and, energetically, it is like a beacon call to narcissists, who can sniff out emotional woundedness like a shark smells blood in the water. Like a chameleon, narcissists expertly morph who they are in order to "match themselves" with damaged emotional patterns in their victims; they can morph into Prince Charming in a hot second – and be whomever or whatever the victim wants him to be. He, therefore "clicks into" her emotional woundedness; she falls "madly in love with him" and, once she is hooked on him and dependent on his love and approval, his nastiness is revealed; his devaluation phase starts.

Emotional memory is a complicated issue that needs more attention than I can give to it in this book. To learn more about it, read my book, Tapping into Love, which discusses the impact of emotional memory in both romantic relationships and one's overall life view.

She knew he would be so very lost without her! Boy had suffered a terrible childhood, which is why he behaved like this.

Making excuses for the narcissist's harmful treatment is done to address the cognitive dissonance that is created from it. Blaming the narcissist's childhood is a popular notion that is actually 1000% spot on: generally, narcissists are made, not born. Dominant, overbearing parents who are also overly-doting, yet emotionally absent, set up their child to develop Narcissistic Personality Disorder - or at least shades of narcissism. HOWEVER! A bad childhood is no excuse or reason for a victim to tolerate mistreatment. If no one ever holds the narcissist accountable, he will never, ever be able to square off with (said) childhood issues, and his (and her!) life will be utterly wasted. He won't stand a chance at breaking down his formidable ego, in order to access his scared, lost, and suffering inner child.

She knew that she was put in his life to help him break through the walls he had built around his heart. She couldn't let this pettiness get in the way of her mission to rescue him from himself.

Here Stump downplays Boy's abusive behaviors to "pettiness." If Stump truly did want to help Boy break through the walls he had built around his heart, she wouldn't patronizing him, acquiesce to his maltreatment, or throw a blanket of forgiveness over him every time he behaves badly.

Furthermore - and this is a trap that many empaths fall into – it is never appropriate to proclaim yourself as the hero of someone else's life story. Stump making it her "mission" to rescue Boy from himself is not coming from love, but from deep fear that he won't "make it" - whatever that means. It is much more empowering and healthy to recognize that Boy showed up in her life to show Stump her own inner wounds - so she has an opportunity to heal them. Keeping her focus on Boy is hugely counterproductive on every level - for both of them.

"I would grow you more apples, Boy," Stump said lovingly. "Better, more delicious apples. But... do you remember? I gave you my branches to build a house."

Stump is continuing her efforts to distract Boy... and gently remind him of her selfless, loving act of giving him her branches. Does Boy care? Does it make him appreciate her more? Abso-freakin-lootly NOT! It just gives him more ammo to garner narc supply.

Boy gave Stump a look of indifference. He shifted his gaze back to the ground. "God, my butt hurts."

Here Boy uses indifference (the polar opposite of love) and distraction; he goes back to his original shame-inducing line about his ass hurting - again, implying that she is too hard – and makes his displeasure with her known. Acknowledgement of her selflessness and gifts to him, something he knows is important to her, will never commeth.

"Tell me about your house, Boy..." Stump said, trying to again distract him from his uncomfortable sit.

Sadly, Stump's efforts to please him continue:

"Oh, God. Why? You know a storm took that piece-of-crap-shack from me long ago. Your wood was porous and weak. I should have known you'd give me bad wood to build my house."

More lies, more projection... and another devastating blow - stating that Stump's wood was weak and porous and that this was the reason for his house being destroyed in the storm. Of course this wasn't her fault! To make sure she is sufficiently distracted from any potential rebuttal against his glaring untruths, Boy immediately throws another zinger in his accusations. "I should have known you'd give me bad wood to build my house." Obviously, this suggests a precedence or history of being disappointed by Stump - which he hasn't been - except in his own pathological projections. His statement has the potential to send Stump into a mental panic and doing a fanatical mental inventory of every interaction she'd ever had with Boy to see if ANYTHING she's ever done could have been interpreted as purposely hurtful to Boy. Note, however, that she doesn't quite buy it. Yet.

"Whaaaat?? You lost my branches?!" Stump blurted in horror.

"Oh Brother. Here we go! Always gotta be nagging at me for something!"

Deflection: blaming Stump for nagging gets him out of the hot seat. It doesn't work initially, however. But he keeps at it.

"But those were my branches, Boy! I needed them to make leaves and apples!"

"Then why did you give them to me?!

"Because you needed a house! And I love you, Boy!"

"Well you sure don't act like it!" Boy's retorted.

Deflection, word salad.

"Don't you get it?! I lost my house. I became home-less. Because your branches SUCKED, and you knew it. You wanted to get rid of them and offloaded them onto me."

This circular discussion keeps Stump's feelings from ever being heard or acknowledged and is the cruelest form of abuse. There is no hope here; Boy will never own up to the truth, because admitting any amount of guilt would be unbearable to his false self. The exception would be, of course, if Stump up and leaves him and moves on with her life. Then he might come crawling back with his tail between his legs, apologizing and asking for another chance. How easily stump gives in to his hoovering will dictate how quickly he goes back to wearing his ass-hat. It's not a question of if - -but when he will put his ass-hat back on.

Stump was in utter disbelief. *Offload them onto him?* How could he possibly say that? Her branches were a tremendous gift to Boy. She missed them terribly. Her life had become grueling since giving them to him. She no longer had leaves to soak up the sun, produce chlorophyll, change colors in the fall, or dance in summer gale. It was an awful thing to be a tree with no leaves. Or branches. The only thing that gave her comfort was knowing that Boy had built a beautiful, sturdy house with them and was enjoying the comforts of his own home, which was built with the superb wood she so lovingly gave him.

Boy knows this was important to Stump that he recognize her generosity and selflessness. But he would never concede to this – unless he was trying to get something else out of her. At this point, Boy views stump as practically worthless, so he has NO reigns on his maltreatment of her.

Boy effectively smashes this "comfort knowing" of Stump's to bits and lets her know that her precious gift to him of all her branches was absolutely wasted. No remorse, no apology, no recognition of how painful this would be for her... only blaming and shaming her for his own irresponsibility.

Yes, this is truly how narcissists behave, think, and conduct their lives.

"I had to move into my parents' basement after it fell down." Boy jeered. "I wish you hadn't brought up such a terrible memory, Stump."

Due to Stump's rebuttal and disbelief, Boy ups the ante with accusations and shaming tactics. Of course, she did NOT bring up the painful memory of Boy needing to move into his parents' basement. In fact, this is the first she's heard of it. Since moving into his parents' basement brought up his own frustration and shame, he needed to project it somewhere other than on himself. Blaming Stump serves double duty, as it also gives him huge, delicious spoonfuls of narcissistic supply.

Stump, again, felt deeply ashamed, even though she knew Boy wasn't remembering the truth about her wood. She didn't offload anything onto him! He had asked her, rather desperately actually, if she could give him a house. She didn't have a house, but generously offered him her branches in order that he may build one. How was Boy he not remembering any of this correctly? Also, he had never told her about his house falling down or needing to move into his parents' basement. So how could she have known not to mention it?

Note the complexity of deceit, manipulation, and blame here. Most victims will just "let it go" because it's just too much effort to untangle the crazy; they've learned that the accuser will never concede anyway. Confronting him or trying to correct his faulty perception only leads to more frustration, more abuse, and more crazy-making discussion. So they just let it go. This is how narcissists are able to continue their abusive patterns; they never need to face any consequence.

Boy continued. "You talk a good game, Stump. But all you want to do is twist the knife with your, 'oh boo hoo, Boy! Those were my branches!' Why would you even say something like this to me, Stump? That was my house Boy's voice cracked with emotion — a skill he had been able to perfect over the years. Fooling Stump into believing she was the one who was being insensitive would win this argument. Booyaahh! It worked. Stump instantly felt like shit, and had no rebuttal.

Stump felt dreadful about making Boy sad. Maybe she really was being selfish?

Stump's shame doesn't seem to make sense: if she knows he's lying, why would she feel ashamed? Remember that emotional memory wounds get triggered - and the reactions often don't make sense.

He was obviously upset about his house falling down. Who wouldn't be? Maybe this was why he was blaming her for giving him bad wood. But... gosh! This was sheer absurdity! She knew her wood was of excellent quality. She reminded herself that Boy had a difficult childhood and she needed to cut him some slack. He was her soulmate, after all. They had a very powerful soul connection. In spite of how he acted, she knew he loved her too. She just knew it.

More cognitive dissonance... more rationalization in attempt to close the ever-widening gap between her beliefs and the cruel untruths that Boy was presenting. The "soul connection" that Boy refuses to recognize is not based on soul, but on her unrecognized emotional woundedness.

Stump knew that her only choice was to forgive him and let it go. It really wasn't THAT big of a deal... right?

WRONG! Oh my goodness, Dear Stump! This is a very, very big deal. Boy was lying, insulting, and manipulating Stump. Her acquiescence and compliance rewarded his ego for these destructive and damaging behaviors, which only increase the likelihood of them happening again.

When she calmed herself down and was able to swallow her truth to a manageable level, she spoke. "Boy, I care about you so much! Please forgive me for not giving you good wood."

Whoop! There it is! Boy wins. Boy sucks. Boy conquers. This is one of the most tragic lines in the whole story. She "swallows her truth to a manageable level"... then asks HIM for forgiveness. With a normal person who understands that forgiveness is a natural ebb-and-flow in a relationship (minus the fact that that Stump was taking the blame for something that wasn't actually her fault) this would be fine, and two healthy adults would discuss the matter in a respectful and mutually beneficial way. But... saying this to a narcissist? It's extremely counterproductive, damaging, and enabling, Blanket forgiveness is devastating to the psyche of the victim, and glorifying and enabling to the narcissist. Boy, by the way, thinks Stump is a pushover and idiot for her pathetic attempts at keeping the peace in the relationship.

Boy shrugged. "Don't worry about it. It's in the past."

Not only does Boy NOT extend any gratitude for Stump's incredibly selfless act of giving him her branches, he refuses to acknowledge his horrific accusations. He lets Stump take the whole blame, then dons the "good guy" cap by telling her "Don't worry about it. It's in the past." So... what truth got swallowed by Stump here? All of it. Who suffers? Who's given the green light to continue his abusive behaviors? Is this ultimately helpful? Ultimately loving? Ultimately Christ-like? Is the emotion behind Stump's passivity true love? Or deep fear?

Although he would never, EVER admit it, Boy absolutely knew that Stump's wood was extremely sturdy and strong. In fact, at the time, Boy couldn't believe his good fortune... that Tree would just GIVE him ALL of her branches!

Narcissists view opportunities to exploit others as "good fortune."

Especially after he had been such a jerk to her! After she gave him all her apples, he just dumped her without any explanation. That was great fun!

*This is an example of **ghosting**. Ghosting is meant to send a victim into a panic and allows the narcissist to garner huge amounts of narcissistic supply (a.k.a.: ego boosts!)*

She kept calling him and being all sweet... trying to figure out what she did wrong.

Boy enjoys and feeds off of the attention and desperation from Stump.

Of course, he never gave her any explanation as to why he didn't come around anymore. This made her freak out and get desperate. Predictable. *yawn!*

Her desperation came in handy though! He was able to get her branches off her for nothing!

Narcissists are opportunistic by nature; they see nothing wrong with deliberately manipulating others in order to exploit them. They have no guilty conscious about this whatsoever. The only time they cry or apologize is if they are caught doing something illegal or know they know they are in deep trouble.

Of course, his stunning good looks had something to do with it. Women couldn't resist him, and he secretly knew it.

Narcissists believe they have superior looks, intelligence, talents, morality, spiritual gifts, etc... and they are, thus, better than others; this gives them permission to exploit others.

Women couldn't resist him! This chick, Stump, was so desperate for his approval that she would do ANYTHING to get it.

While Stump treasures this relationship, in Boy's mind, Stump is reduced to simply being "this chick."

Obviously, Boy would have been a total fool not to capitalize on this opportunity.

Narcissists see other people as disposable commodities. Here is another peek into Boy's opportunistic, parasitic nature and rationalizations for treating Stump so poorly.

The real problem with building his house was that

Boy didn't really know what he was doing. He was obviously too smart to follow the dumb ol' directions. Once he was done, his house looked like it was built by a band of monkeys who had escaped the clutches of a maniacal zoo keeper... and happened upon a random pile of logs, a jar of peanut butter, and a hammer.

The narcissist never wants (or feeling the need) to follow directions. He thinks he can find a better way... because his belief is that he is smarter than other humans, and can figure things out himself.

Now, in Boy's defense, he had run out of nails half-way through building his house. Because of the yammering wooden wench annoying him while he was cutting off her branches, he ended up spending all of his money that night gambling.

Ever shirking responsibility, Boy projects his pathological gambling habit onto the forever giving and loving Stump.

Thus, he had no money to buy more nails. He ended up using peanut butter and kite string to hold the rest of the logs together. He cleverly propped up the sagging west wall with a toilet plunger. It worked great! *Directions my ass!* He cracked open a beer and stepped back to admire his handiwork.

Believing his own delusions - especially as they relate to his stellar intelligence, skills, and accomplishments is common for a narcissist. Here, Boy convinces himself that he did a great job building his poorly built house. When the consequences inevitably come, they are easily deflected onto others.

The only way a narcissist can be "broken" and "healed" from his zombie-like state is through radical humility – which can only happen with a breaking down of his ego – meaning a psychological breakthrough to the lost and terrified child hiding behind his mask. Such a breakthrough almost never happens; there are way too many empaths / codependents in the world who willingly step in and try to fix the narcissist… which they do due to their own unrecognized childhood pain. As long as a narcissist has someone feeding his ego, telling him he's wonderful, and showering him with attention, he will never get the chance to break through his false existence. By the way, narcissists are extremely depressed underneath it all because they have no access to their sense of self. Empaths may be depressed, but they DO have access to their (albeit often beat up and broken) sense of self. This is one reason empaths are so drawn to the healing and spiritual professions / teachings. They are ever-seeking to heal what they intuitively know is broken within them. Sadly, without awareness of narcissistic abuse, whatever headway they make on their healing journey often gets quickly sucked into its voracious black hole.

Regrettably, using all his peanut butter and plunger to stabilize his house would temporarily put a damper on he and Stella's bedroom romps.

Narcissists sometimes coerce victims into doing REALLY WEIRD stuff in bed. This is a control thing; when the victim concedes, it's arousing to the narcissist, and hugely devastating to the victim. She thinks she's being open minded and giving him what he wants, but, really she is relinquishing her self-respect, which, of course, gives him narc supply.

Yet, he fully intended to buy nails the next day so he could finish the job correctly. He was good like that.

Pfffft! At least this is what he tells himself. Not all narcissists are lazy. Many are extremely hard-working and take incredible care in their appearance and lifestyle. However, they all demonstrate an inability to take responsibility for their own behavior.

It is impossible to embody all "flavors" of narcissism within one story. What I want you to see here is the way narcissists deflect responsibility, grossly manipulate and exploit others, and demonstrate dysfunctional and sub-human thought patterns – as evidenced by the way they conduct their lives.

Then... he kinda-sorta forgot all about it. A couple weeks later, a gusty thunderstorm came along and obliterated his house. *Motherfucker! Damn that yammering Tree and her stupid crap wood!* Sadly, his plunger also got washed away in the torrential rain that fateful day. *FACK!*

Pooor Boooooyyyy....

Stump felt bad that Boy had lost his home. Although it was terribly distressing that Boy didn't remember her wood as high quality and strong, she felt his pain. She pressed the subject gently, hoping he might soften up a bit and she could remind him of the truth about her branches... how much unconditional love she had showed him by giving them to him! Surely he would see it. Right now, more than anything, he needed to know he was loved. "Boy, you know it took me more than 25 years to slowly grow my wood..."

Stump still doesn't "get" Boy's neurotic dedication to her demise. There IS no getting him to admit the truth about this matter - or anything that would point to his own irresponsibility. It's a fool's journey - to take on the narcissist in efforts to "win" or get him to see logic. It won't happen. You're far better surmising the situation with knowledge, facts and reality. That (silent) narrative will sounds something like this: "I'm dealing with a narcissist and his false self. There is no hope here. I either need to radically accept him and this situation swallow my truth and walk on eggshells to keep the illusion of peace… or I need to recognize him as being a dysfunctional and mentally dystrophic person. Should I choose truth, I must be willing to go within to heal whatever it is in me that is keeping me stuck in this impossible relationship. IF I radically accept his behavior and continue to sacrifice my wellbeing and soul, is it worth it? If yes, why? If not, what am I going to do about it?" While you may not have all the answers to these difficult questions, the point of this narrative is to get your brain to start building neurons that support the truth - not ignore it while supporting lies and dysfunction.

"I said don't worry about it!" Boy said gruffly. Obviously, he was doing Stump a huge favor by letting it go. (What a guy... What a guy...)

This is truly how Boy sees it! As empaths, we don't want to believe that he's behaving like this on purpose. But, indeed, he is.

Stump sighed and fell silent. She had intentionally

grown her wood slowly, pulling nourishment from Mother Earth and the sun... for the better part of a quarter-century in order to grow her strong wood. But Boy would never see it or listen to reason. He only ever saw things from his point of view, which was usually skewed in some tenuous way that made her look bad.

Maybe she had missed something? Maybe her wood really **was** porous and weak? She mustn't be so arrogant to think it was high quality and strong.

While this core premise of self-reflection is golden, she is focused on the wrong thing. Rather than try to convince herself of an untruth (in this case, Stump questioning the quality of her wood and then chastising herself for being "arrogant" about it) what she needs to do is ask herself, "Why am I allowing this dishonest, destructive person into my life? What old childhood wound within me recognizes and resonates with this same injustice and dysfunction?"

She would let this conversation go too, out of her love and devotion to Boy, and her commitment to being a good person. After a few minutes, she spoke again, hoping to change the mood to a lighthearted one. She knew just what to say. "Hey... Boy? My wood was porous, so my trunk must have made a fine and buoyant boat. Right?"

Desperately Seeking Stump is still looking for Boy's approval and to prove her worth to him. Beware that this energy plays right into the narcissist's hand and practically begs him to abuse you.

"Jesus! Heck no, Stump! That was actually the worst boat ever. I mean, I carved it perfectly, of course. But your trunk was weak and full of air pockets. We tried to sail to an island

His inclusion of the word "we" here seemed accidental, but was, in all likelihood, intentional and meant to make Stump question, "What do you mean, 'we?'" Is it another woman?" etc...

and it hit a jagged rock. Knocked a hole clean through it. You should have told me your wood wasn't strong enough to be a thin-hulled boat."

Who knows if any of this is really true? As we've already witnessed from Boy, Truth is irrelevant. And also strangely relevant, because his false self wholeheartedly believes what he's saying. His motto is - if it serves him (his false self) its truth.

Now, the boat could be sitting in his shed or docked at a port for all we know. His aim here is to INJURE and DESTROY Stump for the sheer thrill of it in order to garner narcissistic supply. - sourced from her soul. Because the gift of her trunk was priceless and irreplaceable, it is the perfect pilfer for his grave abuse. Do not give known narcissists precious things of yours: they will destroy or exploit them, trivialize their value and your (extremely valid) feelings of loss, then turn around and blame you for the whole thing. Boy's mistreatment of her trunk and then blaming Stump for growing bad wood (again) are two separate but intricately connected injurious statements. Obviously, we won't hold our breath for Boy to cop to any mistake on his part - now or in the future.

"Whaaaaat??!!" Stump felt like a sharp rock had just been slammed through her heart! In a way, it had. "What? My... your... my... your... boat sunk???!!" She was barely able to express her spinning thoughts, as she frantically tried to mentally process what had happened to her precious, perfect trunk. She felt like she had been punched in the heart by a gorilla. She tried, but she couldn't hold in her tears. She softly sobbed as she spoke, "That was my only trunk, Boy! Don't you understand that I gave it to you out of the goodness of my heart?" Boy remained silent. He held no expression on his face, save a hint of a smile in his eyes. "Why didn't you tell me about this when it happened, Boy? I think I deserved to know what happened to my trunk..."

"God! Stop yelling." Boy sneered.

What-what? She wasn't yelling! What is he even talking about? "What? I'm not yelling, Boy!" Stump raised her voice, but still wasn't yelling.

Stump wasn't yelling. She (understandably) raised her voice and was calling Boy onto the carpet. "Stop yelling!" is a simple deflection technique. Boy uses it here because Stump is closing in on him. Since he can't take any measure of responsibility, he MUST deflect it. Telling

Stump to "Stop yelling!" interrupts her thought pattern and distracts her into defending herself. This is a very common – almost overly used deflection technique. THIS now becomes the focus of conversation-giving Boy a minute to think up a way to keep Stump from asking about her trunk again.

"You're yelling while saying you're not yelling?!" Boy asserted scornfully.

"I'm talking louder now because you're accusing me of something I'm not doing!"

"Talking louder is yelling!" He yelled. "You accuse me of all kinds of shit, but you can't own up to yours?

The circular deflection discussion endures, leaving Stump overwhelmed, frustrated and completely invalidated. To the unaware empath, this type of madness could consume her whole life!

How does that make any sense, Stump?"

Well, it doesn't make sense, Boy. But not because of Stump, but because of you.

Stump couldn't take much more of this. Boy refused to listen to her and made everything her fault! She decided to just shut up, because everything she ever said just made matters worse.

But she loved Boy! She needed to figure this out! If he would only listen to her for a minute and stop making such ridiculous assumptions...

Boy knows the loss of the boat is devastating to Stump. Since he doesn't value her feelings, he just doesn't care and, in fact, sees her feelings as weakness, begging to be exploited. Boy's motto is: **injure-minimize-deny-blame-repeat.** *Please note: if you're going to do forgiveness work with a narcissist, don't do it in person. I recommend you see a therapist who specializes in narcissistic abuse recovery. Empty chair work, writing and burning (or flushing) letters, EFT and forgiveness through prayer are effective techniques you can use without engaging the narc's ego. Any forgiveness you offer him in person will be seen as stupidity and weakness and immediately exploited.*

"Jesus Christ. If you must know, I didn't tell you about your trunk sinking because I didn't want you to feel guilty for putting our lives in danger. You know, it's your responsibility to warn people if your wood is low quality. Instead, you sold me on it like some snake-oil salesman."

Here, Boy twists Stump loving gift to him into an insinuation of wrong-doing on her part. These twists and jabs are impossible for the victim to untangle because they are designed to induce deep confusion. Let's deconstruct this rotten sentence from Boy:

1) **"I didn't tell you about your trunk sinking because I didn't want you to feel guilty"** *– LIE: there is no reason WHATSOEVER for Stump to feel guilty. This was never even remotely on her mind… until now.*

2) **"...for putting our lives in danger."** *–LIE: Stump didn't put anyone's life in danger – except her own, by giving Boy her life-giving trunk. Note how he twists his own guilty behaviors and projects them* *onto her.*

3) "...But you know, it's your responsibility..." –Insinuating Stump is irresponsible. Obviously, Boy is the grossly irresponsible one. Again, he projects his inadequacy onto her.

4) "...to warn people..." – She didn't need to warn anyone, because her wood was high quality, and the destruction of her trunk wasn't her fault.

5) "...if your wood is low quality."-it wasn't low quality. Besides, it was a GIFT. This piece also gets lost in Boy's narcissistic translation as a way to let Stump know her "gift" was terribly unappreciated.

6) "Instead, you sold me on it..." This insinuates that Stump pushed her trunk onto him... and she somehow got a benefit out of giving him her trunk. The ONLY thing she got (before this exchange) was the good feeling that comes from doing something loving for another person.

7) ...like some snake-oil salesman." Insinuating Stump cannot be trusted and is selfish, conniving, and sneaky. Obviously, she is none of these things. But Boy? Boy is ALL of these things. Projection, projection, projection! When a gift is unappreciated, and even trampled, we can look to the pearls-before-swine passage in the bible to gain understanding:

"Do not throw your pearls before swine, or they will trample them under their feet, and turn and tear you to pieces." Matthew 7:6

Stump gave her (proverbial) pearls to a swine (a.k.a.: a narcissist) and he trampled her gift and then turned and tore her to pieces.

"What in the heck are you talking about?!" Stump's sadness turned to fury. "I GAVE YOU MY WOOD AS

A GIFT!" Now, Stump WAS yelling... much to Boy's delight. "So you could get away from all of your problems! I didn't sell you on anything!"

Here we see Stump start to mentally break down — due to the ever widening cognitive dissonance gap. Sadly, this devastating emotional and mental state in the victim is actually hugely beneficial and exploitative for the narcissist. Her emotional and mental state indicates that he has successfully provoked her into deep confusion, despair, and hopelessness. Boy secretly relishes Stump's meltdown. Unfortunately, his provocation continues:

"God! Chill out already! You always get so dramatic over nothing."

Here, he throws out three more false, injurious statements

1) *Chill out already!*

2) *You always get so dramatic*

3) *Over nothing*

"This isn't nothing, Boy! You're telling me my trunk was nothing? You're not even grateful for it! And now you're saying I should feel GUILTY for giving it to you? And it's somehow MY fault that YOU almost drowned? When you're the klutz who wrecked it?"

Stump is 1000% right in all of this. But Boy will never concede.

"I know it's hard for you to understand, even short

sentences, I guess..."

Ode to Sarah Huckabee Sanders...

Boy spoke with an exaggerated tone of authority, as if Stump was the stupidest person on the planet for believing what she was saying... which was actually the truth. "But if you would LISTEN— I said I DIDN'T want you to feel guilty, which is why I never told you about the boat sinking. Why do you ALWAYS twist things around?""

*Here we observe more gaslighting and twisting of the truth by **Boy**... into a tangled mess that no one could possibly untangle in the midst of a conversation. Friends and family – people who don't understand narcissistic abuse – generally won't have the patience or insight to listen to a victim try to explain it. It's quickly dismissed, or "balled up" into a blanket statement like, "The guy is just a jerk. Who cares what he thinks?" The only hope for the victim for freedom from such a twisted, yucky mess is for her to cut her losses and move on from the abuser. She must recognize her own woundedness and embark on her own healing journey so she can no longer be exploited like this.*

"Are you kidding me? You stupid fucker!" How dare you blame me for that?! Fuck you! Fuck YOU!!!" Her anger was surging, and she couldn't exactly explain why. All she knew was that Boy was being grossly unfair and outrageously ignorant. As usual!

Two things I want to mention here: 1) don't dupe yourself into thinking that just because you can yell and swear at your abuser means you have any measure of personal power. Any upset you show him – even if it's well-articulated – will only serve his pathology. 2) Do you see why the victim often looks like the abuser in the relationship?

It's worth repeating:

"Do not throw your pearls before swine, or they will trample them under their feet, and turn and tear you to pieces." Matthew 7:6

"God, you're bipolar, Stump." Boy jeered.

More bunk from Boy! (Make it stop!)

One of the perpetual goals for a narcissist is to find a way to project his own guilt and inadequacy onto his victim. It's maddening and disheartening, but you MUST recognize that there is no hope in this relationship. You've been had. That's it. Make your decisions from THIS truth, instead of the one your emotional woundedness is urgently trying to get you to believe. There is no hope of Boy owning up to his lies, manipulations or mistakes. There are only more lies and manipulations ahead that that spin into even bigger horrors.

There is no hope for him finally seeing reason.

There is no light at the end of the tunnel.

There is no mutual agreement.

There is no closure.

His human programming is defective. You must realize what is actually happening; you're squaring off with someone who is mentally, emotionally, and spiritually very zombie-like. The light's on but no one is home. His inner child is M.I.A. The sooner you can disengage from such a person, the sooner you can put your life back together.

How dare this pathetic, whiny, worthless stump question him?! It seems like someone needed a reality check as to who was boss in this relationship! "Look, Little Miss Can-Do-No-Wrong, I'm the victim here. I trusted you, and it nearly cost me my life! Your trunk sunk so fast we almost got sucked down with it! Stella and I needed to leap for our lives and swim to the island! So don't you dare blame me, Stump!"

*We see Boy's sense of **entitlement** in full force here. In his delusions, he is entitled to anything good that Stump has, because, in his mind at least, he is a superior being. Dubbing Stump "Little Miss Can-Do-No-Wrong" is a diversion tactic to get Stump to question her reasons for her arguments. Identifying himself as the victim gives him "permission" to dump on her. Remember – much of this crazy scrambling of truth is subconscious; Boy may or may not know he's actually this mentally ill.*

Dropping Stella's name here is absolutely intentional. He did it in such a way-in the heat of an argument-that he can easily manipulate and deny it later. His choice to drop Stella's name is yet another way to injure her; she suddenly knows there is another woman in his life. By the way, please understand that Boy feels completely entitled to his anger and misappropriation of guilt onto Stump.

Also, I feel compelled to say this to my readers who may think this level of manipulation unfolding in the story "would never happen" or that I'm being over the top dramatic here. I'm not. This is how narcissists treat their victims – and worse! The devastation is very, very real. In fact, Narcissistic abuse is a part of the human condition, dating back to AT LEAST biblical times, and is a huge contributor to the prevalence of mental illness, substance abuse, and all things detrimental that we see in society today.

"Boy! My trunk was not crap, and you know it!"

By arguing with Boy, she continues to allow him to abuse her.

"You're so arrogant!

Projection.

How would you know if your trunk was crap or not?

Word salad and deflection. Of COURSE Stump would know the quality of her own wood!

I'm the one who carved it into a boat — not you.

More word salad. Boy CARVED her wood; via his sleight of language, he insinuates that this makes him a greater authority on her wood that she, who actually grew her wood for 25 years.

And I can tell you for sure that your trunk was weak, full of air pockets, and made a horrible boat.

*Even with bold faced lies such as this, the narcissist will swear to God, swear on the Bible, swear to the moon and back that he's telling the truth. The reason for this should spook you to your bones: it's because, whatever serves his false self (which is **his god,**) is the truth. The REAL truth makes no difference. While you are arguing with a narcissist - fighting for justice and your sanity, he's fighting for survival… of his false self. He MUST consume you — or he will die! (This is how it feels to him.)*

People who behave like Boy are extremely mentally sick individuals. Again, please understand that there is no hope in a relationship like this. You can pray for him and put your faith in God, but stop rationalizing your self-debasement or pretending that it's loving, virtuous, or Christ-

like. It's not. If you enable a narcissist to continue abusing you in efforts to keep the peace or be a good and "virtuous" person, you literally feed his pathology and enable him to continue.

Which is why it rammed into a rock and instantly sunk to the bottom of the ocean!"

Deflection and projection.

Stump was beside herself with anger and deep grief. Boy had a way of making these sweeping junk statements that were so far-fetched; there was just no way to form a rebuttal against them. Like so many other times, his statements weren't adding up. "Boy!" she yelled much louder than she intended to. "You're full of it! If my wood was porous and full of air pockets, it would NOT have sunk so fast!"

No matter how loud she yells or how correct she is, he won't hear her, and he won't concede. So, my darling, please don't waste your precious breath or life force energy in trying

Crap. He hadn't thought of that. Not to worry; he knew how to shut her down: inconsequential blame and tangential discussion... meaning discussion that sounds like he's addressing the issue but he's really just talking around it. He had spent years perfecting his craft, and it had gotten him out of a lot of really bad situations where he would have otherwise had to take responsibility.

Narcissists are always, always deflecting blame off of themselves.

"Geeesh! You can't let anything go, can you?!

Deflection and blame.

Don't ask me to figure out your crazy wood growth!

Word salad.

I don't know why your wood sunk so fast. All I know is I did you a HUGE favor by taking that crappy trunk off your hands. So you wanna shut your pie hole and stop calling me a liar?"

Word salad. Word salad. Word salad. In Boy's mind, his manipulating reality preserves his power, and, therefore, is completely justified.

Stump saw no way through Boy's delusional and twisted convictions that made her out to be the irrational one and absolved him of responsibility. He shoved his twisted accounts of her beautiful and by-gone trunk, along with blame for HIS irresponsibility and recklessness in her face.

She's right; there is no way through Boy's delusional and twisted convictions. The only hope is disengagement and healing yourself and rising above the energetic "frequency" of narcissists. Many empaths have gotten "lost" in the rabbit holes of the narcissist's mind games.

Stump couldn't tell if he really believed his delusions? Or if he was just making them up as he went along?

In essence, it doesn't really matter. Either way, the end result is the same.

Nothing about Boy ever made sense. Sometimes she wished she had never met him.

*Stump could walk away from the relationship at this point, before things get worse. With narcissists, everything can and does get worse if you do not take a stand and take steps to protect yourself from his desire to destroy you. If you can't go **no contact** with an abuser, at least manage your expectations within the relationship until a time you can leave.*

Several silent minutes passed. She was beyond angry and doing her best to breathe through it.

There is a difference between self-righteous anger and moral outrage. Don't get duped into believing you have an anger problem, when, really, you're battling a narcissist!

She kinda knew that she had pressed the issue about her sunken trunk too far. And she felt horrible about dropping the f-bomb.

Inappropriate guilt... keeps her beholden to Boy. Narcissists antagonize their prey until she "snaps" in order to make her look like the crazy one.

She also knew that, because of Boy's abysmal childhood, he didn't know how to take responsibility, and he couldn't help being the way he was.

Victims make excuses for their abuser's behavior, which keeps them stuck in the relationship.

Therefore, she really had no choice but to forgive him and let it go.

False, Stump! There's a much better choice: you could stop seeing him and stop enabling him... which would hugely help you and, ultimately, be a huge gift to him.

Yet... Stump missed her trunk very much, and she just couldn't pretend that she didn't. She was deeply hurt, confused, and frustrated; it was getting harder and harder to rationalize away his behavior. *Ugh. Relationships are hard!*

This paragraph portrays Stump's ever-widening cognitive dissonance gap. Generalizing her struggles with "Relationships are hard!" is her way of rationalizing her decision to stay with Boy.

Before today, she had comforted herself with the belief that Boy was enjoying his time sailing away from all his problems... in her trunk that she had so lovingly gave him.

Victims live with one foot in fantasy - as a coping strategy.

What hurt Stump even more was that she knew Boy's soul was in deep trouble. It was obvious by his delusions and behaviors that something was really wrong with him, and it was her job to help him.

*Like many victims, Stump **does** recognize that something is wrong with Boy. She ruminates in worry and guilt over his plight, having NO substantial grasp on how pervasive and enduring his problems really are, and that nothing she can do, say or be could ever fix it.*

While most other women probably rejected him, Stump knew she was special. She had always been able to forgive and love Boy through all of it, and show him that he DOES matter, that he IS loveable, and that she would ALWAYS be there for him.

The golden attributes Stump ascribes to herself are reflections of the recognition that she is craving from other people.

She needed to help him. God had put her in his life so she could help him, because he never had the love he needed as a child. She could give him that love. She was committed to loving him **no matter what.**

These misconceptions and rationalizations will keep Stump stuck in this dangerous relationship forever – until Boy completely consumes her and unceremoniously discards her. Left unchecked, an empath can develop something called The Messiah Complex; this stems from her ability to sooth, calm, nurture the inconsolable parent in her childhood. This gives her a feeling of omnipotence. This sets her up for "finding" the sick and suffering partners. The sicker he is, the more ardently she holds on to her belief that she can "fix him" with her "special powers." This is why so many empaths pursue spiritual healing methods, such as Reiki. Narcissists cleverly capitalize on this propensity in victims in order to garner attention, healing, sex, food, whatever he wants from her. Her freedom comes when she realizes that it's not necessary, required, or appropriate to "fix" anybody. Rather, empaths can hold compassion for and honor the lessons being learned by the suffering person.

She didn't share these thoughts with friends or family anymore. They were all angry with her and held so much judgment toward him! No one understood her deep love for Boy. It's true that Boy was horrid to her most of the time. She knew she tolerated a lot from him.

Here is an example of cognitive dissonance: Stump knows Boy is rotten to her and that she tolerates a lot from him. Yet, she maintains the delusion that Boy loves her. She also pines away after him and claims to love him.

At times she wondered WHY she still loved him. Sometimes Stump wished she could just get over him like everyone told her to. But she didn't know how.

There are a billion people at least whose souls are currently "in trouble" like Stump claims Boy's to be. Yet, Stump has very little interest in "saving" these many other souls from their harrowing fates - just Boy's. This quasi-noble assertion that she must unconditionally love Boy in order to save him is actually one big fat subconscious rationalization that "allows" her to continually feed her emotional addiction to Boy. The disparity of her inexplicable addiction to him and her desire to "just get over him" are typical of those enduring narcissistic abuse, and, yet, another example of cognitive dissonance. She doesn't know how to get over him because her answer doesn't exist with him, his approval, his behavior, or his actions. It exists solely within herself. Healing her original wound is the only way to transform her addiction to Boy, but to guarantee that she no longer attracts other men just like him.

Something else Boy said had the potential to break her heart even more than knowing her trunk was sleeping with the fishes? Stump took a deep breath. "Boy, who's Stella?"

"Stella? I don't know. Why?"

"You said you and Stella had to jump off the sinking boat and swim to the island..."

"I never said Stella."

Denial... denial... denial... Remember that Boy said "Stella" intentionally in his earlier rant.

"Yes you did, Boy. I heard you, loud and clear."

"No, I didn't. I said... Fella. Fella is my dog."

Word salad.

"You have a dog named Fella?"

"Yes, I have a dog named Fella. Open up your ears."

Denial, word salad, gaslighting. Boy lies, gaslights, then blames Stump for not opening up her ears.

"And you took him on the boat to an island?"

Stump isn't exactly buying his story. This greatly annoys Boy.

"Yes!" Boy raised his voice. "Yes! Why is this such a complicated subject? I took my dog on the crap boat with me to the island. I find it unbelievable that I just told you I almost drowned in the sea and my dog had to drag me to shore and island natives had to revive me and all you can do is ask about the name of my dog! What on earth is wrong with you?! Are you PMS-ing or something?"

False narrative, word salad, denial, projection.

Let's analyze this rant. First of all, Boy DID say "Stella," not "Fella." What's more, he did so purposely, but is pretending he didn't. To the narcissist, language is like a game of chess; he gets three steps ahead of his victim (whom he's studied and knows very well). Boy KNOWS that Stump will obsess about Stella, and he pretends he said her name absentmindedly, and then denies even saying it. (Again, don't try to figure it out why... it's all about acquisition of power and control in the relationship - and narcissists play very dirty, and devoid of all sensible rules.) Secondly, he didn't say he almost drowned. He said he (and Stella) COULD have drowned - which, of course, is an exaggerated truth in and of itself. Obviously, he never said his dog drug him to shore or anything about the island natives reviving him. Insinuating that Stump is insensitive because she somehow "missed" these details in his conversation is another stroke of gaslighting. Another comes when he accuses her with "all you can do is ask me about the name of my dog" which took the entire conversation out of context, railroaded right over Stump's very legitimate questions, put her on the defensive, and had her questioning herself as to whether or not she was hearing Boy correctly. "What's wrong with you?" is a rhetorical question that is built on the premise that Boy is making valid statements (which, of course, he's not).

Do you see why knowledge of narcissism is so important? Look at the amount of effort and words - from me - someone who understands narcissism on many levels - needed to put into this explanation in order to untangle Boy's flippant rant. There is no way that a victim who isn't aware of these tactics could possibly do this in a real-life situation, in real time, while inundated with her own emotions, and while it was actually happening. Her emotional triggers would be far too great. Even if she did manage to do it, the narcissist would continue to fire his torpedoes, keeping her in a consistent state of anxiety and confusion.

Whuuuut did he just say? That he almost drowned? And in the same breath, insinuated she didn't care? Then blamed it all on her PMS-ing? What? Just... what??

Weaving gross and sweeping lies with threads of truth is an effective way to confuse Stump and make her feel guilty.

Stump was, again, faced with a whirlwind of non-sense that she felt powerless to counter. There was nothing to do here but forgive it and let him know she cared. "I'm sorry, Boy... I didn't hear you say that you almost drowned..."

Again, no accountability, for Boy, swallowing the lies, taking blame that isn't hers, and giving him the go-ahead to continue abusing her.

"I said it! But you never listen!" Boy retorted.

False narrative, deflection...

Stump sighed. Boy was just being his impossible self again. Sadly, it was nothing she hadn't witnessed or forgiven before.

Stump is resigned to Boy being "his impossible self." This is a dangerous mindset, and, you should know, if you find yourself in a similar circumstance, things will only get worse - never better between you and the narcissist.

But Boy really was so angry and convicted about all this... so he must be telling the truth... from his warped perspective.

The narcissistic rages and convictions can be very convincing to the victim of his grossly invalid points. As long as a victim is confused, she can't take action... which is exactly where Stump is, and exactly where Boy wants her.

Maybe he is just this confused? Maybe he really thinks I don't care that he almost drowned?

No, Stump; he doesn't think that. That's his guilt hook, getting you to doubt yourself. Self-doubt is often the result of these exchanges, as Boy offers zero space for authentic discussion and remains resolute in his stance.

But... he knows better! There were so many unanswered questions, and she never seemed to get any straight answers.

This is the quintessential narcissistic conversation: it goes in circles and never goes anywhere. It only serves to give more opportunities for the narcissist to impose his injuries on the victim.

Maybe if she spoke very gently, he would listen. "Boy, I've missed you so much... and I don't remember you ever saying you had a dog named Fella... or that you almost drowned... and I just want you to be honest with me about Stella..."

Stump still believes she is dealing with a rational person, with rational reasoning ability, and a mutual desire to heal their relationship. She has no idea that all of this "crazy" has been purposely orchestrated by Boy's twisted, maniacal mind in order to control, manipulate, and ultimately destroy her.

"Oh, quit your yammering, Stump! I'm sick of you going on and on and on with nonsense. We've talked about this for 20 minutes. Can we be done with it?"

Boy reduces Stump's concerns to "yammering." Narcs are famous for dropping these lines during arguments, especially if the victim presents some very valid points and backs him into a corner. A narc will pretends that you've already talked about (whatever it is) when in reality, all he's done is squawked all around it and your very legitimate concerns. If someone uses this line with you during a disagreement and you still have many unanswered questions, pay attention. You're probably dealing with a narcissist - or at least someone with tendencies toward it. As the discussion continues, the victim soon gets labeled a "nag" and the narcissist triumphs… again.

"But Boy, you didn't answer any of my…"

"PLEASE??!!" He yelled gruffly, as if he was very put out.

Ohh…. poooor Boy! He needs to deal with Stump's ridiculousness!

Stump fell silent.

Confusion, compliance, silence. Sadly, it's the victim's way…

Boy went on a self-pitying rant of embittered grumbling. "Mrfsgegerf damn it… hermb ererergerm eferber…I haven't ererergermeseen you in fermescur years rmererergermefe….I'm rmescuhalf hour and you're hermedederbrrmehjerscreby back to rmescu same incessant nagging. I jererergermefet here and have a nice rest rmescu spend time with you, ererergermefe ruin the peace and quiet mescur bederme foot-stool wannabe…"

This is embittered grumbling rant is a way for Boy to let Stump know that he's justifiably angry (he's not - except in his own mind) and to keep her in a state of anxiety. Boy grumbling angrily under his breath keeps her on edge, walking on eggshells, and utterly miserable – right where he wants her. There is no hope here. Boy will never concede. He will never change. If you find yourself in a similar position, I officially give you permission to walk away from this relationship and reclaim your life! If you don't feel ready to walk away, or if you are somehow enmeshed or dependent on the narc, simply bring this to your awareness. Making a conscious decision to stay in an abusive relationship – versus an unconscious one – is, ultimately, far healthier in the long run, as our goal is to get you to own your life, your decisions, and your life direction.

Stump said nothing. This was maddening, unfair, and awful! Yet she had faith that Boy would one day break through his anger and see who she really was: a kind, forgiving, supportive person who loved him with her whole heart.

Since Stump's forgiveness and unconditional love are serving the narcissist's false self, this "breakthrough" will never, ever happen through her efforts. The only glimmer of prayer a narcissist has of ever breaking through his false self is if he were to actually suffer the consequences of his behavior and actions. If no one in the whole world fed into it, he would crumble, his false mask would get ripped off, and the terrified, shrunken, cowering inner child within him would be exposed - and given a chance to heal. Therefore, enabling a narcissist through blanket forgiveness perpetuates his evil - and not, in any way, helps him, you, your children, or society.

Truth be told, she was actually a little desperate. Nobody else would want her at this point. She had no apples, no leaves, no branches, no trunk...

Besides exploitation of resources, low self-esteem is a consequence of narcissistic abuse. What gets damaged so badly is the victim's perception of reality and, therefore, an inability to trust her own knowing, which leads to the drastic diminishing of her sense-of-self. Every time she tolerates abuse, sweeps it under the rug, or throws a blanket of forgiveness over an unapologetic abuser, she gives him a piece of her soul.

Even a very short time spent with a narcissist can do incredible personal damage. Give up your fairytale of him ever being who he was in the beginning, during his love-bombing phase - or anything more than he is right now. Don't try to get even. Don't try to get him to change. Realize you are entangled with a person with sub-human "programming," who is very dangerous to your wellbeing, your children's wellbeing, and the wellbeing of those you love.

...she had given all of these things up to this man she loved.

Again, this "love" isn't love - it's an emotional memory response.

God had put her in charge of saving Boy's soul,

Wrong! God doesn't put people "in charge" of saving anyone's soul - especially if it means losing yours in the process.

giving him everything that ever meant anything to her was part of the rumble. She mustn't question it.

Thick and dangerous rationalization here.

In spite of all of her flaws, and the fact that he was so mad at her all the time, she knew Boy loved her very much.

You hear this from victims. "I know he loves me, in spite of his mean, gruff exterior." This is indicative of a deeper childhood wound – one involving a (probably) abusive and emotionally absent parent. To the developing child, being loved by a parent is psychologically crucial. If a parent fails to show the child love, the child will strive to fill this CogDis gap with rationalizations and blanket statements. I.e.: "I know s/he loves me!" This is the exact pattern that is showing up in her relation-ship today – with her abusive, emotionally absent partner, Boy. Resolving this requires that Stump to go to her logic and square off with the truth of it. How is he showing her love? His actions, words, demeanor, and history show a blatant pattern of disrespect, manipu-lation, and indifference to her pain. This is not love, by any stretch.

She was worried about him. He was so fragile and always had such terrible things happen to him. Like his house falling down and his boat sinking.

Boy's "bad luck" is an effect of his unwillingness to take any measure of responsibility. Stump's unconditional love and support is being fed to a very hungry, very dark, very evil entity called narcissism.

Of course he blamed her; it wasn't safe to blame himself because of his bad childhood. Stump knew that he just could never make it in life without her unconditional love and support.

*Well this is at least partially true: his **false self** could never make it in life without her unconditional love and support. But, as previously discussed, upholding his false self is dangerous and counterproductive for them both... especially if she is truly worried about his soul. What would help Boy more than anything is allowing him to fall fully into the pain of his own consequence. In order to do this, Stump needs to step back and stop feeding the beast within him.*

Stump couldn't bear the thought of him ever being with another woman. While it seemed he might have been, it was easier to just let it go and give the whole situation to God.

Jealousy, insecurity, and fear of abandonment all spring from Stump's unmet, unrecognized emotional (childhood/teenage-hood) woundedness. This is exactly why wounded people can become morbidly jealous, obsessed, manipulative, and stalker-ish with ex-lovers. In Stump's case, she chooses to put blinders on, in favor of a quasi-Christian approach to "give the whole situation to God." This is because prior displays of jealousy or obsession with Boy left her painfully broken. It's easier to throw a big, web blanket of forgiveness over it, give it to God, and pretend everything is okay. Chicken shit karma – in the making!

She knew that she mustn't let her imagination get carried away with her on this Stella thing. He probably did say Fella. She just heard him wrong. Like always. She sighed. "I'm sorry, Boy."

More rationalization to fill the gap of cognitive dissonance, and more internalizing Boy's manipulation and dysfunction, which, of course, he quickly capitalizes on:

"You get on my last nerve, Stump!" Boy lifted his hat and smoothed back his thinning salt-and-pepper hair. "Even Tom and Harry agree with me: you're impossible!" He replaced his hat.

This is an example of "phantom" triangulation. The fact that Tom and Harry don't actually exist is irrelevant in Boy's mind. Narcissists often create supporters out of thin air in order to harass and embarrass victims. Of course, narcs will also triangulate with real people - these are often people who have very little contact with the victim and, very often, are unaware they are being used by the narcissist in this way.

"Who... who are Tom and Harry?" She asked timidly.

"Tom and Harry! You know? The guys I play squash with. Jesus! You don't remember a thing, do you?"

More lies and deflecting back to Stump's alleged ineptness.

Boy knew Stump would be mortified about Tom and Harry - who didn't actually exist. Distracting Stump with the idea of Tom and Harry was his best bet to get her off this Stella rant — which he, of course, had invoked on purpose. Later she would realize he never gave her a direct answer, and she would toss and turn all night because of it. Ha! Dumb bitch. *Oh yeah! Mega heartbreaker in da house, y'all!*

Here we see Boy's mental "chess game" in action, which is played against Stump's sanity. Sadly, because Stump is virtually dying for his love and approval, he uses her as a pawn in his own game against her.

Stump was mortified that Boy told Tom and Harry that she was crazy and impossible! Why would he do that? She wasn't crazy OR impossible! She was nice! She was giving! She was kind! But Tom and Harry could only know what Boy had told them about her. How could she make this right?

You can't... except by realizing you are being used as a pawn in a very sick and twisted mind game. Your only chance of making this right is by recognizing the truth of your situation and relationship with Boy.

She knew that if she were able to talk to them, she could explain this misunderstanding. But she knew that Boy would never let her meet them. She never got to meet any of his friends.

Even if the triangulated third party DID exist, Boy has set his version of the story up in such a way that there will be no redemption for Stump. Anything she says can and will be used against her in the court of narc.

What it all came down to was this: she needed to regain Boy's respect. But she wasn't sure how to do that. The only thing she could think of was that she needed to go on a really strict health kick to get her body back. A protein shake and daily exercise would help her regrow her trunk, branches, and apples. That way, she could give Boy more apples and wood. Then he'd be in love with her again. Yep! That's it. She'd start tomorrow.

Stump is internalizing Boy's grave dysfunction. (How can I regain his respect?) She never had his respect in the first place. In the beginning of a narc relationship, there is the love bombing phase, which has the narc doting on and adoring the victim, but this is a ploy – used to hook her into his pathology. What's more: anything Stump creates of value will be devoured by Boy's voracious narcissistic appetite. Let's suppose that Stump IS able to miraculously grow a new trunk and branches - and become who she was pre-Boy. If she does not do significant healing work on her original woundedness, Boy - or someone else very much like him - will come right along and gobble up all of that goodness for himself.

A few years ago, she had decided to take her life-savings and get herself a trunk implant. She ended up canceling her surgery last minute and giving the money to Boy; he needed to buy a new car because his old one somehow ended up at the bottom of a lake. (Pooooor Boooyyy!!!) She needed to help him!

Again - no consideration for the fact that she needed a new trunk and that this was Stump's life savings; he learned about her stockpile of money and coerced her into giving it to him – probably with promises to pay her back, which he never does, nor has any intention of doing.

She finally heard him sigh and felt his bony butt relax. Thank God. It would be safe for her to speak again, as long as she didn't mention Tom, Harry, Stella, Fella, the boat, her apples, her branches, her trunk, or anything else that Boy might interpret as upsetting or weird.

This paragraph demonstrates Stump's hypervigilance. It indicates how much control Boy has over her. Stump is scared to have a normal conversation with him because he might jump down her throat again... which is hugely painful for her. Rather than telling him to bug off and realize that she's dealing with a control freak, she buys into his judgments, internalizes his ridicule and incorporates it into her perpetually dwindling sense-of-self. Stump's focus is on him - the outside world, rather than herself - the internal environment because she is scared of crossing the impossible and constantly shifting lines that he's drawn for her over the course of their relationship.

Sadly, she couldn't think of a single thing to say.

Silence is extremely uncomfortable for the codependent. This is because she is almost 100% externally focused. Therefore, the lie is - silence = no external feedback coming in = no "me" being reflected back... which feels invalidating and scary. Pay attention to how comfortable you are with silence. If you feel uncomfortable with it, try bringing your focus back within you.

But the silence was deafening! She needed to say SOMEthing! "Your... butt feels nice and relaxed, Boy."

"Huh?!" Boy lifted his head and furrowed his brow. What the... hell is that supposed to mean?"

Stump was embarrassed.

By embarrassing her, Boy is able to extract narcissistic supply from her.

Actually, this was ridiculous. She was getting really tired of feeling this way. Truth be told, she was exhausted with this whole walking on eggshells bit that he had reduced her to... even though she didn't actually have feet. Heck, maybe her family and friends were right. Maybe she deserved better. Maybe Boy was just a grumpy, miserable man who was using her during his dry spells.

Here we see Stump's logic and truth peeking through Boy's tangled mats of deception and manipulation. This can happen when abusers push their victim "too far." Narcissists have a sixth sense about their sources of narc supply "going there" and are naturally spiritually on guard; Stump getting wise would cut him off from being able to suck her soul dry. It doesn't take long for him to regain control.

These thoughts hurt her heart. But Boy's attitude toward her was simply unbearable anymore. For the first time in a long time, she started to entertain the idea of ending their relationship. Stump went deep into thought, wondering how exactly she would tell him that she just couldn't see him anymore.

Here we see Stump contemplating the ending of the relationship. Even though she doesn't say anything to him, Boy senses it. He feels her backing up, and that he may have pushed it a bit too far. This is why, in his next line, he hoovers her and pulls her right back in:

"Isn't this a pretty day?" Boy asked cheerfully, as if no awful, manipulative or degrading conversation had just taken place between them.

Not only is Boy's sudden cheer a hoovering tactic, it is actually another extremely subtle form of denial. A sudden cheerful attitude is hugely confusing and, of course, extraordinarily invalidating to Stump because the horrendous things Boy said to over the course of this conversation are suddenly off-topic, and obviously not a concern of Boy's. Sadly, Stump falls right back in line without a hint of resistance:

Huh? Stump was brought out of her deep thought by

Boy's unexpected cheer.

Boy's sudden cheer also creates cognitive dissonance - because there is no identifiable impetus for it. Again, the name of the game for the narcissist is confusion, degradation, and life-force-energy extraction. Like a soul-ninja, he has moves that his victim never sees coming. Sudden cheer is one of them.

She finally responded. "Oh. Oh! Yes! It's so sunny!" She spoke in the happiest tone she could muster. She was grateful for Boy's change of mood.

The other thing sudden cheer does is create gratitude in the victim. Sudden cheer is used to disarm a victim who is "getting wise." She is so grateful for this reprieve from his normally abusive treatment that she quickly forgets "all that bad stuff" and, being the kind, loving, forgiving person she is, falls in line far too quickly.

She knew this was because she was so forgiving, and he was finally breaking through all the pain around his heart. (Hooray! Praise Jesus! Hallelujah!) "I love these crisp, sunny days with you, Boy."

No, Stump. He's not breaking through all the pain around his heart... this is all manipulation of your kindness and hyperactive empathy. Sorry to say, Darling, you've been had - again.

"Yep! We've shared a lot of them together... 'ey Stump?" Boy gave her a pat.

Continuing his hoovering - reminding her of wonderful times.

"Indeed! We've had so many fun times, Boy." Stump was enjoying this unanticipated moment of nostalgia with him. She signed deeply and smiled to herself. The love and faith in her heart quickly returned.

The sun was shining just for them in this moment. Ahh! The sweet sun! How she missed the days when she could bask its generous warmth, contribute to the precious oxygen stores on the planet,

As conscientious and social beings, we must be able to contribute to the good of society. We thrive when we do so. We whither and corrode when we don't or can't. A narcissist strips his victim of her ability to contribute to society, and all of the benefits of doing so.

with Boy resting comfortably in her branches. These were some of the happiest memories of her life. How silly of her to think that Boy was just a grumpy, miserable man who was using her during his dry spells. Nothing could be further from the truth.

Sadly, because of Stump's weak resolve, one moment of kindness from Boy sucks her right back into his claws. A woman with high standards and healthy self-respect doesn't build relationships out of a partner's intermittent kindness and respect.

He loved her. And she loved him. This moment proved it.

Stump got a bit choked up on her feelings of the moment.

The reason a victim often feels so emotional in moments of emotional connection with the narcissist is because he momentarily is satiating the emotionally starved child within her. In such a state, the unexpressed tears of childhood race to the surface. The ego then constructs a false reality around these feelings that feel like truth. In Stump's case, the false reality is "He loved her. And she loved him. This moment proved it." This feels very real, and in such a state, the victim is extremely vulnerable.

Sadly, this caused her to speak without thinking. "Oh, Boy! I wish I still had my branches so you could climb up and hide in me and forget about the world." Stump stopped short, realizing she had just uttered words about a touchy subject: her branches. "Um... I mean..."

Boy has "trained" Stump to not discuss anything that explicitly or implicitly makes Boy look guilty.

"God, you just had to bring it up again, didn't you?!" Boy yelled.

Stump's alluding to the fact that she missed her branches and leaves was a big no-no with Boy! She was not allowed to suggest anything that may paint him in a bad or guilty light. Further, any joy, gratitude, or trust in the relationship must be immediately squelched by Boy. It's the narc's way!

"I'm sorry, Boy... I didn't mean it was your fault..."

Rather than receive an apology from Boy (which she deserved) she apologizes to HIM! (We see this in dysfunctional partnerships in many relationships – not just romantic ones.)

"Whatever, Stump. You're always trying to make me feel guilty for something.

Projection; he is the one always doing this to her.

When are you going to face the facts? Your leaves are gone. Your apples are gone. Your branches are gone. Your trunk is gone. Just... friggin' deal with it! And stop making me out to be the tyrant in this relationship!

Obviously, Stump never made Boy out to be a tyrant. He did that all on his own. However, this statement from him gives us a glimpse into the truth about how he sees himself. He both projects onto Stump and blames her for his own guilt and agony. This behavior is very typical for a narcissist. It's one reason that some things they say seem to come out of left field, out of context, and make no sense. If this happens, start thinking "projection of his own crap, followed by blaming me for his own crap." *ugh... exhausting, isn't it?*

God! Do you have any idea what I have to put up with from you?"

More projection…

Stump felt scrambled and devastated. She strived to

be the most loving, docile, easygoing person she could for him, but it wasn't easy. She knew that Boy couldn't help the way he was. He just couldn't. She needed to try harder to bite her tongue and extend compassion — and not get so angry with him. Poor guy. *I'm such a bitch!* Her heart sunk into shame.

Remember, even though none of this is her fault, Boy, being a narcissist, is able to intuitively "hone in" on Stump's deeper woundedness and exploit it. Therefore, even if it makes NO sense, she will take on the blame, and then react with shame, self-depreciation, and doubt.

How was it that she tried *so hard* to be his every-thing, yet she was constantly reduced to nothing? All of the beautiful parts of her were gone. She had given them to him, trying to make him happy. But no matter what she gave him, it wasn't enough, she was always messing up... and she was always empty.

Stump doesn't consider the fact that Boy is mentally unstable, with no desire to fix anything in the relationship.

Boy never apologized for hurting her feelings. Yet she was always apologizing to him — even for the stuff he did. She always tried like crazy to make things right.

Nothing will ever be enough for him... because Boy's soul is virtually a vacuous pit of emptiness, darkness, despair, and hopelessness. The arrogance and grandiosity he portrays are projections of his false mask

166 The Giving Stump

that he's put in place of his sense-of-self. No amount of apples, branches, tree trunks, money, fame, food, sex, possessions, or anything else will fill his void. It isn't until his mask is shattered and he's broken on the ground that he will suffer enough to actually choose do something about it. Therefore, every action that enables the narcissist (like unconditional forgiveness while closing a blind eye to his tyranny) pulls him further away from God / Divine / Source and, therefore, is not at all virtuous.

Stump comforted herself with the pearls of wisdom she had heard from her wise elders over the years:

"Love means never having to say you're sorry."

An expression certainly invented by narcissists – who never say they're sorry!

"Unconditional love means we look past our loved one's flaws to their good underneath it."

Unconditional love does not equate tolerating abuse or enabling their dysfunction.

"True love conquers all."

True love *does not enable dysfunction. True love throws consequence in its face, with faith in the other person's ability to transform - should he choose.*

"All you need is love."

Not exactly true! In order to survive, we also need food, and shelter, and money, and clothes, and water, and respect, and safety. All of these life necessities are threatened when you become entangled with a narcissist.

"Love is the answer."

Again, what we are witnessing between Stump and Boy is not love. Love doesn't acquiesce to or encourage abuse.

Stump took a deep breath and told herself she was NOT giving up on Boy or their relationship.

By not giving up on their relationship she gave up on herself.

"I'm hungry," said Boy. "I sure could go for an apple right now."

This comment is meant to twist the knife - especially considering their earlier conversation about her "wormy, rotten apples."

Stump slumped.

Stump is becoming resigned to Boy's abuse - a signal that Boy has been successful in "breaking hers spirit" and sucking her soul dry.

"Oh yeah..." Boy grumbled.

A rude and purposeful dig at Stump…

Boy sighed deeply. Several silent moments passed until he casually leaned back on his hands and crossed one foot over the other. He started to hum a cheerful tune: User Friendly, by Marilyn Manson. Stump was confused by his return to cheer, but grateful he was no longer angry with her.

Changing up moods is a manipulative tactic that narcissists use to keep their victims confused and on "high alert."

Boy spoke in a happy tone. "It's so weird how you and I are actually dating. Don't you think, Stump?"

"Why? What do you mean, Boy?"

"I don't know," Boy said nonchalantly. "Maybe 'cuz I usually date women with bigger boobs and a nicer ass than you."

Absolutely intentionally injurious to Stump's feelings. There is nothing innocent in this statement, and no way to interpret it except that it was a purposeful insult, meant to upset Stump.

Stump was flabbergasted. "Boy, why would you even say such a mean thing to me?!"

A very legitimate question, Stump! Unfortunately, Boy isn't right in the head… and you responding to him with upset only plays into his hands and intentions to degrade and demoralize you.

"Huh? What? <insert dumb and confused look here.> I'm just saying that I usually date women with bigger boobs and a nicer ass. Why do you always have to take everything so personally?"

"Huh? What? I'm just saying…" said while playing dumb is extremely typical for narcs. He then repeats what he "was just saying"– in order to get in another dig. Then, in the same breath, MINIMIZES

*what he was "just saying" and faults the victim for her (very normal) upset. This is followed by his attempts to coerce the victim into changing her mind about what she's perceived in what "he was just saying." This sordid scenario is extremely common with narcissists, and, actually, why some psychology experts believe that narcissism is a form of autism – as there is an (expressed) marked lack of social awareness. While those afflicted with true autism are genuinely unable to navigate social cues, and will thus say inappropriate or offending things because of it, narcissists just **pretend** they don't get it-out of a desire to inflict harm. This misnomer by our psychology professionals is a horrible insult to autists!*

*Be very clear – no matter how "dumb" a narcissist plays, he absolutely DOES get it. How do we know? Just this: narcissists can morph into extremely charming, benevolent, and loving people on a moment's notice (people with autism cannot, and have no desire to be fake. Boy's cruel statements here are very **purposeful** and calculated: two things an autist would never be able to (or want to) execute. Autists are extremely honest by default. Narcissists are extremely dishonest by default. While an autist may be truly confused when another is upset with him, the narc plays dumb on purpose, in order to add insult to injury.*

"I would never say something like that to you. That's so rude!"

"Oh, now I'm the rude one? Seriously, Stump? I thought you had better self-esteem than that. I can't even make a simple comment without you freaking out."

Gaslighting, denial, deflection, blame shifting… referring to his remark as "an innocent comment" is also a form of word salad.

Once again she was angry and deeply hurt. Why would even **think** to say something like this? Then not understand why she was upset?

It never crossed her mind that Boy said it on purpose and was playing dumb.

He must have been kicked in the head by a donkey or run over by a rogue carpet cleaner as a kid. Any normal person would be able to SEE how hurtful this comment was. How did he not get it?!

No one has ever taught Stump about narcissistic abuse! If they had, she would understand why Boy behaves this way. Being utterly perplexed and contemplating reasons for his completely inexplicable behavior is common for victims; she doesn't have a paradigm for such utter nonsense in her brain, so she starts going to suppositions. "He must have been run over by a rogue carpet cleaner as a kid" makes more sense to her than his behavior ever will. When these don't add up, she turns to the only other place that makes sense —herself. Which is exactly what Stump did here:

She then wondered if, indeed, she was too sensitive and was freaking out over nothing.

Stump turns it around in her own mind to be her fault. This is likely a reflection of "survival" behavior she learned in childhood in efforts to allay the anger of, and, thus, stay safe from an abusive parent.

She just didn't know anymore. If she were to be really honest with herself, she knew she had let her body go over the last few years... to the point he may not be as attracted to her.

Very sad... See how quickly Stump turns it all around and blames herself? One of the reasons victims do this is because they are subconsciously trying to regain control of their lives and the perpetual problems in it and try to take personal responsibility in finding a way to remedy it. This is admirable, but, of course, futile.

Maybe this is just his way of trying to subtly drop the hint? She decided to forgive his misstep.

Rationalization – to fill the CogDis gap: Stump reduces Boy's abusive and detrimental insults and lack of empathy to a "misstep."

He was probably right: she didn't need to take his comment personally.

*Wrong, Stump! He was probably wrong! Stump continues to buy into Boy's feigned ignorance. Typically, the victim self-reflects and genuinely tries to see her role in the "misunderstanding." While this is normally a healthy practice, in narcissistic relationships, the victim is the ONLY one doing self-reflection and working to come to a better understanding with the partner. Narcissists are incapable of self-reflection in an argument – because, quite literally, there is no **self** to reflect upon.*

A minute later, Boy stood up. "I need to take a dump, Stump. Can you give me a toilet?"

Some narcissists (certainly not all) run over personal boundaries by overly discussing bodily functions. This is a fairly mild statement here by Boy – and as far as I go in this book with this concept. However, know that you may be dealing with a narcissist if he tells you all the sordid details of all things grotesque about his physical body. A lot of this is for shock value, followed by pretending its normal. You'll know how big, how long, how smelly, and whether or not his turds float. He'll talk about oozing sores, toenail fungus, and jock itch. Or he'll scratch himself right in front of you, then go eat without washing his hands... then tell you, "You sound like my mother!" when you point it out to him. The level of "disgusting" can reach ridiculous levels. The antidote to this is self-love and (silent) standards, which translate into effecting healthy relationship boundaries.

"Boy, I don't have a toilet. I'm a tree stump."

Due to his grandiosity, Boy believes everyone needs to cater to his every whim, urge, and desire. He also sees NOTHING wrong with pointing out other people's flaws - which, by the way are almost always his own projections. Because he takes no responsibility for finding his own toilet while he's out in the woods... visiting a tree stump, he projects his own ineptness onto her. Beware of this: narcissists love to create impossible situations like this to see how high they can get victims to jump.

Stump felt ashamed by her lack of toilet-ness. "I'm sorry, Boy. I wish I could be better for you..." She knew Boy was getting ready to leave, and she would spend many lonely days waiting for his return. But she had no idea how to make him stay... or how give him something that she didn't have.

"I gotta walk a mile and a half up the road to take the browns to the super-bowl, Stump. If you want me to visit you more often, you need to get a toilet." He started to walk off.

Boy hammers on the impossible ultimatum that he just put on Stump to provide him with a toilet. He then uses this same "flaw" of hers as his excuse for not visiting her.

"Boy, wait!" Stump cried.

"What now, Stump?"

"Um... I... um..." Stump stammered. "Well, Boy, maybe you... you can carve me into a toilet."

Stump is so desperate to fill this need for Boy - to become, behold, beget something she simply isn't - that she willingly sacrifices the little bit of herself that she has left. Trees are not supposed to be toilets. But this steadfast life-truth makes no difference in her effort to become one. Boy has become her God. Boy replaces the truth of even Mother Nature.

Boy stared at Stump in disbelief. His silence made her nervous.

Everything Boy does makes her nervous... Her "nerves" are triggered by a primal gut instinct because... HELLO! He's dangerous!

"I mean... um...," she stammered. "If you want to, then you wouldn't need to walk so far to use the bathroom."

Stammering for his approval... still. Sad.

Boy brought his hand to his chin and contemplated Stump's odd proposition. Though he didn't lead on, he felt an excitement that she hadn't that she hadn't ignited in him in a long time

Like a drug addiction, it is arousing to a narcissist to have opportunities to garner narcissistic supply from victims. Victims mistake this arousal as rekindled connection and love from the narcissist.

The first time he felt this primal excitement was when she let him take her apples after his "oh, boo hoo! I don't have any money!" story. He thought THAT was a thrill. But then, she let him take her branches, which she was stupid enough to give up for him after his "boo hoo! I don't have a house!" story.

That excitement was only outdone by his "Oh, Tree! I'm so sad! I need to get away... in a boat!" story... and she let him cut down her trunk – a trunk that took her 25 years to grow – just so he could slam it into a jagged rock the first time he and Stella took it out on the water. HA! *Stupid wench.*

Narcissists get off on harming others. Again, this makes no sense to you and me. But narcissists don't operate from normal, rational, empathic realities. If it isn't quite clear to you yet, they aren't normal humans with normal thinking. A narcissist's one and only goal in life is to uphold the grandiose, false self. He does this by destroying others - so he can feel comparatively superior. This is why they are purposefully deviant, destructive, and dangerous.

Stump had just handed him a golden ticket for the

thrill of the century. This whole "you can carve me into a toilet" proposal was horrible, cruel and downright disgusting... and far too good to pass up! "Well... shut my mouth, my Little Apple Tart! That's actually a great idea!"

"It... it is?"

"Yes! It is!" Boy pulled out his pocket knife. "You're brilliant! It's a very, very good idea!"

Tossing her a breadcrumb via the compliment, "You're brilliant" is a purposeful manipulation here.

"Okay..." but Stump was suddenly unsure about it.

Here we see another example of cognitive dissonance. This is the same process of self - degradation that causes anyone to willingly "sacrifice" a part (or all) of him or herself for another. Now, this is where it gets freaky. In Stump's case, her conflicting cognitive dissonance thoughts/forces are:

1) "I want to please Boy, and, thereby garner the love and approval I crave from him. (This, remember, is due to her childhood woundedness and is entirely subconscious) In order to do this, I need to let him carve me into a toilet."

2) "I don't wanna be carved into a toilet!! Whaaaahhhh!!!" It's obviously counter to Stump's survival instinct and LOGIC to allow someone to carve her guts out with a dull knife... so she can be a toilet... in order to fulfill an invented "need" for him.

Which "force" will "win" this internal war? You would THINK it would be #2. However, #1 is borne out of her deep woundedness- woven into her survival instinct in the first place... which means it perversely "hi-jacks" (said) survival instinct in order to overpower the real and present danger - Boy standing there with his knife in hand.

In order to transform this devastating cognitive circumstance, Stump must first become aware of what is actually happening: that her neurological, biological, and hormonal systems have all been hijacked in the name of Boy. She needs to do the inner work to identify, heal, and transform her woundedness. In this way, she can remember who she truly is and move back into who she truly is- an integrated, congruent, self-respecting and centered being who is aligned with TRUE unconditional love. From such a space, enabling Boy's raucous, callous abuse would be impossible. And, certainly, allowing him to carve her guts out would be inconceivable.

"Stump, if I carved you into a toilet, I could visit you every day," Boy spoke gently and assuredly.

Notice how he hones in on her deepest desire – which is always related to her woundedness - in order to gain her trust.

"You could?" Stump asked, taken aback by Boy's sudden kindness. "Every day?"

Pure manipulation...

"Yes! Because I wouldn't have to walk into town to use the bathroom."

Stump wanted, more than anything, to believe him. Boy had stopped visiting her every day a long, long time ago. Could this bathroom inconvenience be at the heart of his decision to stay away from her?

Because Stump does not have a mental paradigm for Boy's illogical and terrible behavior, she is consistently looking for logical ways to explain it. This falls into the CogDis category – and the rationalizations that victims create in response to it.

Deep down, Stump didn't believe Boy would really visit her every day, even if she let him carve her into a toilet. But she was so desperate that she would even settle for a once-a-week-after-a-six-pack-2-a.m. visit from him. But even that seemed like a tall order for Boy.

This paragraph shows how Boy has worn away Stump's standards. Soooo many women (and men) in the world today suffer in this same way. They succumb to the detrimental, life-changing manipulation out of pure desperation for love and approval.

Yet, Boy was older now. Certainly, at this point in his life, he realized there wasn't another woman alive today who would love him as deeply as she did. Surely he realized that that life without love was not worth living at all. Surely he realized that Stump was the BEST thing that ever happened to him. Where else was he going to find someone even half as generous, kind, and loving as she was?

Sadly, Stump is still trying to convince herself that Boy loves and appreciates her. She analyzes, compares, creates suppositions, and, essentially, in efforts to address her original wounds, occupies every single neural pathway in her brain in trying to conceive a plan to help him magically morph into the man of her dreams. And, of course, he never will.

Boy loved having this much control over Stump. He could manipulate her into doing just about anything. Lately, she had become boring; there was very little left to exploit in her, thus very little left to feed his soul. But this? Literally carving her guts out? He was highly aroused just thinking about it. Just wait 'til the boys at the Titty-Tushy Tavern hear about this!

Sadly, it's not just gambling that sucks up Boy's money and resources, but also strip joints, pornography, and all things sexual. This is a common, sad fate for many (though not all) narcissists. Why? Boy's false self is his only identity. Nothing about himself is observed with an internal locus of control. This means that he ONLY identifies himself through his external environment. Therefore, the only way he can relate to women is to objectify her. Does she have a nice rack? A nice ass? What does her face look like? Will she make my friend's jealous? Will she make my dick hard? Can she sufficiently get me off? Does she have money? Prestige? Will she make me look good?

This is NOT an exaggeration. It is honestly how a narc sees women, and how he "measures" a woman's worth. His romantic life pursuits are nothing more than desperation to fulfill the emptiness within him. Boy has no connection to his heart, no understanding of true love, or reverence for any quality besides physical beauty, money, hedonistic pleasure, and prestige. Qualities like compassion, intelligence, kindness, integrity - are all expendable, exploitable, stupidible weaknesses that have no business in his romantic partners. Because of this, a narcissist will sometimes troll strip clubs in search of physical perfection, and pay bookoo bucks to women who measure up to his unrealistic ideals. He will express repulsion and distain for women who don't. ALL of it is a reflection of his own deep and pervasive emptiness.

Stump then caught sight of the pocket knife in Boy's hand. She shuddered. "Um Boy, you don't intend to use that tiny, dull knife to carve me - do you? That will hurt too much."

Ahh, crap. He was looking forward to slowly scraping away her insides using a dull knife. He wasn't used to resistance from her. The stumpy tramp! Time to up the ante. "Oh, come on, baby! It won't be bad. I'll be gentle."

Patronizing, minimizing, and rationalizing. Rather than feeling genuine compassion or concern for Stump and the pain she might feel, Boy's focus is on, "How do I get my way?"

"No, Boy... you need to use a better knife."

Although Stump didn't normally stand up for herself, this was a glaringly obvious problem. As the story continues, however, we observe the process of Boy using Stump's compassion and deep craving for his approval against her, and crumble her resolve.

Boy was miffed. He didn't have a better knife! Not with him. How dare she inconvenience him?

Never mind the fact that his plan to carve her into a toilet might actually inconvenience her. (This thought process is completely rational to the narcissist, by the way.)

Luckily, he knew just how to sway her resolve to his favor. "Stump..." boy's demeanor was suddenly solemn. "I've got a confession to make."

Here we go...

"What?" Stump was curious. "What is it?"

"I understand why you don't want me to use this dull knife. Even though it's the one my grand-daddy gave me from the Civil War... right... right before he died." Boy wiped an imaginary tear from his eye.

Eliciting pity - especially through shallow feeling, almost colloquial assertions that tend to have "sweeping" qualities - like this one. In this example, Boy saying, "... the one my grand-daddy gave me from the Civil War right before he died" is not something that can be easily challenged or debunked without coming across like a heartless jerk.) This is a problem for empaths and codependents who thrive on approval from others. A narcissist uses these tactics to mine a victim's empathy in order to leverage his desired outcome.

Huh? This was very strange talk coming from Boy. "You do??" Except in the beginning of their relation-ship, Stump never heard any form of understanding compassion, or sadness coming from him. *<insert twilight zone music here.>*

"Yes, my love. I know what it's like to have dull pain in your gut."

Here we see an example of hoovering - trying to pull her back in so he can re-hook her. He also sets up his hook to relate to Stump's fear of pain from having her guts carved out by a dull pocket knife.

"Oh..." Stump's heart blipped with delight upon hearing him call her "my love." *swooon...*

Aaaaannd she's re-hooked. She has no real clue how easily he's playing her. Keep in mind: he does ALL of this manipulation in order to achieve his end goal – which is to be able to carve her with his dull knife.

"You see, the reason I haven't been able to visit you very much is because I have irritable bowel syndrome. I was diagnosed with it years ago, and, well, I need to be very near a bathroom at all times, or things could get messy."

"Oh no! Boy, I'm so sorry to hear that!"

I call this "reverse deflection." Boy successfully gets the focus OFF of Stump's upset about his dull pocket knife and onto his (fabricated) illness. The fact that his illness can essentially "mirror" the pain that Stump will feel from having her guts carved out is not coincidental.

Awesome! She's buyin' it! "Yeah. My... um... my guts hurt a lot. I'm so embarrassed, I didn't want to tell you... because... because I didn't want you to fall out of love with me..." Boy managed to get real tears in his eyes.

Here, Boy is mirroring Stump's fears. "I didn't want you to fall out of love with me" is a direct path into Stump's psyche - which will bring a flood of empathy and "feel good" emotions from her - which will ultimately make her decision to let him carve her guts out with a dull pocket knife.

"Oh! Boy! No! Don't ever think like that! You can tell me anything!"

*Yeah, she bought it... as predicted. *yawn**

He took off his glasses and set them and his pocket knife down on Stump. "Will you hold these for me, Baby?" He asked in a quivering voice.

All acting... and yes, narcissists become highly skilled at mimicking emotions and knowing just what to say to re-engage a victim.

"Of course, Boy..." Stump didn't like to see Boy cry. But she was overjoyed that he was finally feeling his emotional pain. He was so sad inside. "Let it out, Boy. I'm here for you."

Stump moves immediately into the overly-doting, nurturing role... pathetic, pallid, and predictable. Ugh...

He pulled out a handkerchief and cried into it. He wiped his eyes and blew his nose. "Oh, Stump! You're just so understanding, kind, and loving!"

Here he is telling her all the words she's been craving to hear. Boy knows where Stump is "starving" emotionally, and wields this knowledge to suit his agendas. He KNOWS that him seeing her as "understanding and loving" is very important to her. She's been letting him cut off all the parts of herself trying to prove it. He has steadfastly refused to say these words to her... until now. Now, however, he is using them as leverage for his end game.

*Important! Since Stump is virtually starving for Boy's recognition, love, and attention, his words **feel** genuine and true. Her survival instinct (WARNING! WARNING! Don't let crazed man with dull knife carve you into a toilet!) is drowned out in her tidal wave of "joy" – which is a chance to satiate her decades-old, subconscious emotional memory pain of never having the love she's craved her whole life.*

He sobbed into his handkerchief for a good minute before peering over it to make sure she was paying attention. Yep! She was. *Perfect!*

Everything a narcissist does, everything he thinks, every move he makes is in efforts to secure and garner narcissistic supply. Sacrificial lambs like Stump are easy to manipulate because their core motivators are avoiding guilt and seeking love.

He moved his handkerchief away from his face and gave her the most pathetic smile he could muster.

This is important. Narcissists are absolute masters at mimicking human emotions. However, there are telltale signs that these emotions are fabricated. Checking to see if anyone is paying attention is one sign. We will see another in a moment.

She gently smiled back. He reached down and put a hand on Stumps strong, smooth and beautiful wood and rubbed it sensually. "You're amazing, Baby..." he said. He was obviously very moved by her loving support.

Boy's pulls out all the stops here: his touch - which she's also starving for, more of his soft sobbing, and expertly delivered compliments manipulate her. A MOST stellar performance by Boy here! Note: jumping back to the autistic piece: an autistic person would never be able to (or even desire to) quickly calculate these actions and words needed to manipulate his target. The social awareness piece just isn't developed enough for autistic individuals. With narcissists, it IS there but is used "as needed" to benefit his grandiosity and false self.

Stump felt her insides melt from his unexpected touch. Boy had a way of assuring her that everything would be okay... with just the touch of his hand.

Again - this "assurance" she feels is the flooding of her own internal emotional memory being finally, at long last, satiated. The following internal thought process spills forward all of her gushing, fawning, pathetic fairytale pining... along with plenty of rationalizations for his horrific behavior.

Oh, how she had missed him! Oh, how she desired to make him happy! She couldn't BELIEVE he had stayed away because of his silly embarrassment! Although she was sad that he was sick, Stump was relieved to finally have some answers as to why Boy was so resistant to engaging in a healthy relationship with her.

Notice how all of the previous horrors of the day are suddenly forgotten – thrown to the wind as she fully falls into and embraces this "love" she has for Boy.

Stump knew that physical sickness was related to unprocessed emotions in the body. Boy probably had trapped emotions in his intestines - aka dis-ease - from the terrible tummy issues he experienced when he was a kid. His family had no electricity. All he and his family had to eat was jackfruit and jalapeños and they had to light their farts on fire for heat.

A narcissist will tell crazy oh woe-is-me stories to garner pity and manipulate a victim.

Poooooor Boy!! Poor sad, helpless, sick, embarrassed, broken, Boy! How dare she give him so much grief over using a dull knife to carve her? After everything he's been through?! She was determined to show Boy how much she loved him, and how easygoing and understanding she really was. "Boy, I'm sorry you felt like you couldn't confide in me."

Oops! There it is!

"Well…" boy sniffed and wiped his eyes. "You **can** be an insufferable cunt sometimes…"

Boy can't resist an opportunity for a deep jab - at a time he knows she will be less positioned to argue - due to his portrayal of overwhelming sadness. Since Stump's heart is wide open in this "tender" moment, Boy's suggestions, insults, and abrasive comments go in much more deeply – psychologically speaking – than normal.

Stump was shocked. Boy must have said it without thinking. "Boy! I know you're upset, but you can't say things like that to me.

"What? What did I say?" Boy looked at Stump with weepy and confused eyes.

"You know. The c-word."

"Oh. Cunt? Oh, that's not a bad word, Baby. *sniff!* It's… just means a woman who <u>C</u>an't <u>U</u>nderstand <u>N</u>ormal <u>T</u>hinking. That's all I meant, Baby. I wasn't actually calling you that.

Narcissists minimize, twist and downplay the most abasing insults like this and try to get the victim to believe they "aren't meant in a bad way." This serves their thrill-seeking efforts to overtake, manipulate, and devour their victim in any and all ways. If he can get her to accept that she is, indeed, a cunt, she hands over that part of her soul – which he quickly devours. Little by little, he gets her used to horrible insults, and can then dole them out whenever he wants. Eventually, she will simply just take it from him, without so much as a whimper back.

Further, telling Stump that she "can't understand normal thinking" - especially to rationalize his horrid insult - is an example of a layering tactic that narcissists use in order to gravely injure. Such an approach requires extra dedication to feigned ignorance. Games, nested in games, nested in games. The only way to "win" such this game is through awareness, self-respect, and distancing yourself from a person who would behave this way… and going within and healing the part of you that is resonating with such treatment.

What you DON'T want to do is exactly what Stump did: she tried to reason with him. Observe:

"It's still not okay to say that to me. And I **CAN** understand rational thinking. You just aren't fair sometimes."

"Baby, you know you don't understand logic most of the time, but… but I love you anyway." Boy brought his handkerchief to his face and softly wept.

Here, Boy pairs his manipulation with "I love you anyway" – words Stump has been aching to hear from him for a very long time. Instead of saying them authentically, he uses "I love you" as a manipulation in order to meet his morbid goal of getting her to accept the belief that she's a cunt. While extremely subtle, Boy's phrase pairing here is purposeful and meant to disarm her, distract her, and, ultimately, win her over with the idea that calling her a cunt is completely acceptable. His tears disarm her further.

"It's just… this irritable bowel syndrome has really got me lately… and you just don't seem very patient with me over it. And our damn president is such an ass and you don't understand the pressure I'm under just to function day to day. Please don't yell at me, Baby. I can't take it. Not today. I just can't take it!"

Excuses, deflection, and emotional manipulation. Boom, boom, and boom. She concedes. Further, observe that, even with all this emotion, Boy does not apologize. When narcissists DO apologize, it's when their back is to the wall and they are at risk for losing a source of supply. Apologies become part of their hoovering efforts. Narc apologies are more "blanket" apologies, said with false (albeit convincing) conviction and are sometimes coupled with tenderness, affection, gifts, and promises to "be better" or "try harder." The empath, having no idea the level of deviance she's witnessing conceded, and enjoys the temporary euphoria of the illusion of reconnecting with him. Once she is re-hooked, he returns to wearing his ass hat.

Wait… what? How did the conversation go from talking about the C word to the president? Why was Boy crying so hard again? Stump was so confused!

The reason Stump is so confused is because Boy is using word salad, deflection, emotional manipulation, and feigned ignorance to effectively avoid "the C-word argument." Thus, her (legitimate) concerns over his degrading insult (calling her an "insufferable cunt") get completely buried in his crazy. Without an understanding of covert mental abuse, this conversation would confuse almost any normal human being. Freedom from his mania comes when you successfully disengage from him, walk away from any hope of "closure" with him, and heal your own emotional woundedness that is drawing him to you in the first place. It's a process…

"Boy, I know you're upset. But you really hurt my

feelings."

"How?"

"Because you called me that c-word. I would like an apology, Boy."

"I'm not going to apologize for something you just misinterpreted." Boy was still sniffing away, making it clear that he was the hurt one in the equation here. "I didn't do anything wrong, Baby."

Narcissists rarely apologize. When they do, it is usually because they are trying to get something from a victim or gain her trust.

Stump felt sick. She felt angry. How could she argue with this level of ignorance? Especially with him crying like this? She couldn't. She had learned many times over: arguing with Boy was never worth it.

Notice the cognitive dissonance: she realizes that arguing with Boy isn't worth it. But rather than leaving the relationship, she stays, and hopes he somehow "gets" it. Obviously, this never happens.

All was not lost, however. She had grown incredibly strong from all of the unwarranted forgiveness and love she had doled out to Boy over the years. When she looked at it this way, Boy was one of the biggest contributors to her spiritual growth. #soulmate.

Here we observe her rationalizing in order to fill in her aforementioned CogDis gap. We see this kind of rationalization all the time in the current spiritual climates. Get this: a soulmate wearing an ass hat needs to be treated as such. NOWHERE in any true spiritual scriptures or writings of light does it say we must give our souls up for another's injurious behavior that serves his ego. Again, many codependents will don the "unconditionally loving" label and concede (and, therefore, encourage) evil narc actions like this. Sadly, they are always shocked at the pervasive devastation that follows.

Besides, this was **obviously** no time to argue with Boy!

This is the perfect time to argue with Boy! It's the perfect time to tell him NO! Sadly, Stump believes that Boy's mental functioning is normal. She can't possibly fathom his level of pathology. In this way, victims can actually gaslight themselves. This enables them to continue with their engagement with the narcissist, and nurse their unrecognized emotional wounds that are demanding all their energy, time, and focus. They do so right alongside the awareness that something is gravely wrong in the relationship.

He was finally showing his vulnerable side, and she didn't want a silly squabble to ruin it. So she let his horrid comment go, accepted the apology she would never receive, and shifted her focus to the good stuff that was happening right here, right now between them. Boy was still crying; clearly a sign of a big emotional breakthrough!

It's not real. Like the optical illusions that the man behind the curtain fabricated in The Wizard of Oz, none of Boy's emotions are real. This is unfathomable to Stump because nothing in her brain has the (conscious) knowing that another person could ever be so deviant. However, since her own emotional memory is running the show, she is in perpetual pursuit of his approval, affections, and love.

Of course, Stump, being the loving earth angel who was able to forgive everything, knew she needed to do what was best for the relationship. "I'm sorry, Boy, if I've been insensitive to your needs."

"What was best for the relationship" is a poorly defined objective that Stump has created in order to continue her addiction to Boy. In essence, anything that is good for the (narc) is bad for the victim.

"I'm just doing my best, Baby..."

This is a treacherous lie at best...

Boy continued to sob into his handkerchief. All I'm asking for is a toilet so I can visit you more often. I love you, Baby. I love you. I need to see you more often! My life just doesn't work without you. Can we at least agree to that much?"

Notice how he minimizes his intentions with "All I'm asking for is a toilet" as if Stump would be terribly selfish to deny him such a simple request. This masterful play of deflection on Boy's part is hit home once again with his falsely declared "I love you." (Spoooooooky stuff, peeps!)

Stump, too, was overwhelmed with emotion. She had

no idea Boy loved her this much! Upon hearing his sweet words, she felt a joy well up inside of her and the return of her knowing that she and Boy are meant to be.

By now you know the source of her "joy." Her emotional woundedness was being satiated through Boy's outwardly kind words and actions.

She made her decision. "Yes! Yes, my darling Boy!"

(Just in case you're wondering what an emotional decision looks like…)

She whispered lovingly. "Of course you can carve me into a toilet with your dull pocket knife from your grand-daddy, if it would mean that much to you.

The unaware empath can be easily manipulated by displays of sadnes, or any emotional pain, and often jump through hoops, including extreme self-negating ones, in efforts to ease the suffering of others. It's no surprise that narcissists manipulate this tendency in their victims. Offering concern for Boy's (alleged) irritable bowel syndrome is one thing, and an appropriate response. Allowing herself to be carved into a toilet because of it is a decision that comes from a deep woundedness and longing for love and acceptance.

"Yes, it would, Stump. It really would." Boy softly sobbed. "I've missed you so much, Stump, and if we can make this happen, I'll visit you every day." Boy was impressed with his acting ability. "I promise!"

He slyly cinches the deal with a false promise that plays into her aforementioned woundedness.

"That will be wonderful, Boy. I'm in! Let's do this!"

"That's my girl!" Boy exclaimed. Stump felt a wave of joy. He called her *his girl!*

Then... Boy's tears miraculously dried up. His doleful expressions morphed into cold indifference. His loving demeanor abruptly stopped. He stood up, put his glasses back on, and tucked his handkerchief back into his coat pocket.

Here we see more telltale signs of Boy's fabricated emotions. Incongruent emotional missteps that make a normal person go "huuhh? Wait..." Boy's tears suddenly drying up and him abruptly abandoning his overflowing, heartfelt dialogue just doesn't happen with normal adults. It just doesn't. Children, yes. Periods of narcissism are part of the developmental process of individuation. But if this behavior is happening in an adult, don't ignore it or downplay it. It means something.

He stepped back and sized up Stump, contemplating the best way to go about this new and exciting wood working project. He then snorted loudly, gathering the phlegm from crying into his throat, and, with dramatic flair, hocked a huge loogie right next to her. It landed on one of her roots. It felt disgusting, but Stump remained silent, secretly trying to hold on to the euphoria of knowing that she and Boy belonged together.

Boy can't resist delivering a deliberate assault. A narcissist will do things like this this after emotional exchanges in order to keep his victim off balance, confused, degraded, controlled.

He knelt down next to Stump and ran an open hand across her flat wood. "Fuck, yessssss!!" Boy almost hissed. Stump shuddered. His mood was suddenly... aggressively euphoric... which made no sense to her.

An aggressive sense of euphoria is an extremely subtle clue that the person is feeding his "addiction" of inflicting injury onto another. If you think back, you will recognize the presence of this subtle clue in your abuser. Damn spooky. Don't be timid about saying "NO, this doesn't feel right…" should you ever encounter this again!

Stump felt an eerie chill come over her. She suddenly felt deeply afraid, with a stark realization that this *carve-me-into-a-toilet* was actually a really bad idea. But what should she do? She already agreed to it. If she stopped him now, Boy would be so upset, and she would probably never see him again!

Don't mistake "ignoring the obvious" for "positive thinking.'

She began to silently chant *om* to calm her nerves-something she learned to do in her Sunday healing circle. *Oommm... oommmm... oommmm...* and forced herself to think only positive, uplifting thoughts. *This is the least I can do for our relationship. Ommmm... Boy didn't need to tell me about his irritable bowel syndrome, but he did! Oooommm... That must have been hard for him to do! Ooommmm... We love each other. This is all for the best. Ooooommmm...*

Spiritual practice is not meant to whitewash abuse or dangerous situations in order to make you "okay with it" or beholden to an abuser. There's a whole lotta mental calisthenics going on here with Stump's efforts to silence her very normal, very accurate biological fear response. What she really needs to do is say, "NO! I do not agree to this! Go away, Boy!" But, as we can see, she is far too scared of his reaction and that she might not ever see him again. As you now know, this is due to her unrecognized and traumatic emotional memory.

Also, if it hasn't occurred to you just yet, Boy doesn't have IBS. He has MBS: Manipulative Bullshit Syndrome – everything he does and says is done to manipulate Stump into giving up her life force energy, her resolve, her self-respect, and her soul.

Boy scraped his knife across her flat surface. Stump winced. "Oh! Are you okay, Sweetheart?" Boy asked. His gentle touch felt so genuine and soothing.

Sweetheart- my ass! Wake up, Stump! Wake up!

Stump smiled inside. He called her Sweetheart! His gentle touch felt so genuine and sweet; there was just nothing like it in the world. As her heart opened to his affections, her fear subsided. Stump realized that her hesitations about being carved into a toilet with a dull pocket-knife were RIDICULOUS!

Soooo ridiculous, Stump! Whew! You dodged THAT bullet! Again, we are witnessing the power of emotional memory wounds and how they can hijack a victim's logic, survival instinct, and entire life.

Forgiving Boy was easy. He was a very good soul. She felt it. He gave her a deep fulfillment that no one else could ever understand.

This is her emotional memory and her desire to heal it talking...

She knew that her selfless, loving act today would show him, once and for all, how much she truly loved him. Her love would melt his angry shell, blast his heart open, and he would finally own up to the truth about how much he loved her. No one else could see it. But she just *knew* it.

No amount of self-depreciating, "martyrialistic" love will EVER blast Boy's heart open. Ever... ever... ever. This flavor of love, it turns out, is an imposter! Stump's actions here fall under the category of "enabling" and only serve to grow the beast within Boy... his false self within him. Don't do it, Puddy!!

"You are the perfect size and height for a toilet."

*Ohh... **STOP** it, you silver-tongued devil...*

Hmm... not the most flattering of compliments, but it was a start. Though the scrapes from his knife were excruciating, the feel of his hands on her as he brushed away the wood chips sent blissful tingles throughout her roots. As Boy fell into a cadence of carving and smoothing, Stump was lulled into an inexplicable euphoria.

Here we are witnessing the phenomenon of trauma bonding. Significant pain and significant pleasure neuro-biologically firing together powerfully bonds a victim to her abuser. This is due to her neuro-biological interpretation of such a person (one who brings pain with pleasure) as "this is a very important person!"

In her euphoria, she started daydreaming about her and Boy's wedding. She saw the whole day very clearly: a bonafide fairytale. She knew that, on a soul level, their wedding had already taken place. In fact, it surely existed in a parallel reality – or on some other plane, because her visualization of it was just so real! Yay!

When a victim's physical reality is in ruins, there is a tendency to "escape" to dreamy, spiritual realms. I've done it, myself! This is NOT the same as existing in an integrated soul-mind-body state - which is productive and healthy. This "escaping to spirituality" is exactly why we see so many broken people in spiritual circles as healers, readers, and dreamers etc... without even realizing they are broken. If you've ever gotten a Tarot or Angel Card reading from a broken psychic, you probably felt more confused, upset, despaired than you did before the reading. This is the kind of thing that gives spiritual practitioners a bad name. Use your own knowing. If you heal the wounds within you, no one can throw salt in them, hook them, or exploit them.

None of this is to denounce spiritual principles, but rather, to raise your awareness of the importance of integrating them into a life that belongs to YOU - not an abuser. Strive to create a life worth living... rather than escaping.

A spiritually healthy individual integrates spirituality into her physical reality that is built on self-respect and healthy boundaries. Here, Stump is clearly using spiritual "realities" which are really escape pods for her abysmal life which, at this point, has been almost fully appropriated by Boy.

A spring wedding would be lovely: perhaps mid April when the other trees were dancing with blossoms and wildflowers were bursting to life in brilliant, juicy colors.

More escaping, more dreaming of unrealistic circumstance. The psychological term for this is dissociation.

However, Stump was realistic.

Ch-yaahh! TOTALLY realistic!

She knew that she was a little too stout to wear taffeta, which tends to add pounds. Velvet would be too hot for a spring wedding and also had a tendency to add girth to a bride. Satin or silk in a pale ivory would bring out the natural color of her bark and accentuate her features beautifully.

She would need to start her guest list right away! Sadly, she had been out of touch with her friends and family for many years. It all started because, for some bizarre reason, Boy began telling dreadful lies about her... and they believed him. He said she was mentally ill, acting crazy, abusing him, doing drugs and drinking, neglecting responsibilities, taking his credit cards and spending his money, sleeping with other men, something about a plunger fetish... None of it made any sense. Why would he say such awful things about her? It was quite perplexing. She figured he was projecting traumatic memories about his mother, who was nuts. So naturally, she forgave him.

This is what's called smear campaigning and perpetuating false narratives. As a means of gaslighting and gaining mental control over a victim, a narcissist will occasionally spread lies, twisted truths, and deep-dark secrets– which he typically finagles out of her during the love-bombing phase - by the way. Here, Boy spreads lies about Stump for the soul purpose of triangulating her own family and friends against her.

A narcissist can be VERY convincing and present well thought out and methodical false narratives that are difficult for the victim to refute. The triangulated third party is rarely, if ever thinking "narcissist / false narrative / smear campaign against my loved one (because WHO in their right mind would do such a thing?). This leads to secondary abuse, also referred to as secondary gaslighting; the narc easily convinces a once dear friend / family member that the victim is somehow pathological or abusive – and s/he believes it. The friend or family member then starts treating the victim with suspicion, distain, and disrespect. The victim's rebuttals and explanations hold no water, for she is no match for the narcissist's pathology. The narcissist comes across as the victim, and isolation from family members for the true victim results.

However, she was so distressed over the loss of her friends and family she decided to see a psychiatrist. Miraculously, during this time, Boy really stepped up and said he wanted to do his part to heal the relationship. He accompanied her to her therapy appointments and even wanted to have some sessions by himself with the good doctor. **Obviously,** if the relationship wasn't important to Boy, he would have never done any of this. At last, Stump was hopeful!

*If **it isn't obvious,** Boy accompanied Stump to her psychiatric appointments to triangulate the unsuspecting doctor against her and to further his own agenda. This is a classic move for narcissists… and, unforgivable for the doctor! Psychiatrists, psychologists, therapists, and all mental health care practitioners need to be aware about the realities of narcissistic abuse, and are responsible for not imposing tertiary abuse onto their clients.*

"Miss Stump," The doctor told her solemnly one day. "All couples go through misunderstandings and trials.

You seem to have a skewed perception of, and a very pronounced emotional response to normal, everyday events. I've gotten to know Boy these last few weeks. He would never try to hurt you, or tell lies to your family." The doctor seemed deeply concerned. "In fact, if I didn't know better, I would say you are the one abusing Boy – not the other way around."

Boy has clearly skewed the reality of what's going on in the relationship. He has successfully turned the doctor into a flying monkey.

Stump burst in to gut-wrenching sobs. She had never felt so completely humiliated, invalidated, and misunderstood in all her life! "Doctor, that's not true! You're wrong! Boy, he... does all kinds of crazy stuff! He... he hides my keys and pretends he doesn't know where they are. He deletes my favorite songs off my playlists. He steals my peanut butter! He's the one spending my money! He told terrible lies about me and turned my family against me! You've got to believe me, Doctor!"

"It's not a matter of me believing you. I'm just highly concerned.

This is word salad on the doctor's part. What does that even mean? Of COURSE it's a matter of him believing her. And, being a professional, he should at least consider that narc abuse may be the true culprit here.

"Boy also said that you belong to a cult?"

"WHAT?" She almost yelled. "I go to a healing circle every Sunday! It's not a cult! It gives me peace!"

"Well, from what he's described, it sounds highly suspicious."

Narcissists often (subconsciously) despise any type of healing or spiritual group that gives the victim contact with others who may catch on to what's going on in the relationship. And many times narcissists triangulate others – like the good doctor here – to do their dirty work for them. Remember, readers, no matter how bad it gets, or how many people seem to be against you, the truth is the truth is the truth. Do not sell yours to the devil over "confusion."

Stump was utterly baffled. The same frustrations, and demoralizing discussions she's had with Boy over the years was now taking place with a highly trained professional! How could this even be? Unless... unless... maybe she really WAS crazy?

This notion was soon confirmed by the good doctor. "Miss Stump, you seem to be a bit paranoid and suffering from a distorted sense of reality." He then prescribed her anti-psychotics and anti-depressants and sent her to a weekly therapy group for crazy people who couldn't get a grip on life. The pills messed with her head. Three weeks later, she ended up in a psych hospital. THAT was a rough year!

When anti- psychotics and ant-depressants are prescribed to people who don't actually have organic brain disorders, psychosis results. Doctors should rule out narcissistic abuse before prescribing them!

During her stay at the hospital, she learned about healthy relationship boundaries. She realized that she crossed Boy's boundaries all the time! Rather than yelling or swearing to communicate with him, she needed to exercise compassion and patience. Above all, she needed to speak calmly and stop nitpicking him to death if she wanted this relationship to work.

*This horrifying scenario in Stump's past depicts what's called **tertiary abuse**. Tertiary abuse occurs when a therapist or other health professional(s) don't believe the victim and either minimizes her concerns or, worse, blames her for the formidable difficulties in the relationship. Not surprisingly, if the counselor has any communication with the narcissist, he will become ensnared in the falsehoods, deflections, and lies, and, thus, become triangulated against the very client he is supposed to be helping. Think about it: from his perspective, Boy is cool as a cucumber, and Stump is an emotional wreck who is always screaming and swearing. Who looks like the crazy one? Who looks like the victim?*

As Richard Grannon explains (in the same video I quoted at the beginning of this book) tertiary gaslighting forces the victim to "swim in a soup of moral relativism, where they don't know up from down and don't know right from wrong anymore." (Exactly, Richard! Thank you for calling this out so perfectly!) Therapists, psychologists, and doctors are not all knowing, all seeing gods. Be cautious about blindly believing them, especially if you feel invalidated, misunderstood, and re-victimized after your sessions. In some cases, therapists, themselves, are narcissists!

*The overarching cure for this maniacal, mind-scrambling, soul-sucking condition is **reclaiming and healing your authentic sense of self.** I will cover these processes in the next three volumes of The Stump Diaries.*

Thus, with the help of therapy, Stump was able to heal her life. Kinda-sorta. She still felt like shit about herself. She felt even more hopeless. She still felt jumbled. But she was finally able to let go of the past and forgive Boy for the things that he didn't really do, and still wasn't really doing anyway... or something like that. She hoped her family and friends would one day realize that she was just going through a difficult time back then, and whatever happened between them was probably just a big mix-up.

Victims of narcissistic abuse are routinely isolated from their family and friends by manipulative actions of the narcissist. Triangulation between the victim and her family members, gaslighting to make a victim believe that certain family members or friends are somehow a menace or detriment… all of this happens in the abuser's efforts to isolate his victim and keep her from obtaining support or logical perspective of loved ones.

She knew the wedding would be a glorious time of

healing and love for all!

These grand leaps – from reality to fantasy– are common for people suffering with Complex PTSD. This is essentially a subconscious coping strategy that, unfortunately, sets them up for more ridicule and abuse.

Her pain was in the past now, and she would not think of it again! *After all, she thought, all we have is the present moment!*

Victims and survivors need to beware: trite phrases and "words to live by" do NOT absolve the horrors of narcissistic abuse. In order for these "present moment" wisdoms to be applied in a healthy way, you must correct the way you relate to life, yourself, and your reality. Do not use them to forgive or whitewash perpetual abuse, no matter how tempting it is or how encouraged by others you are to do so.

Boy was going to make such a handsome groom! She could just see him in his dashing tuxedo, cumberbun and bow tie. *sigh!*

Stump is escaping reality and overriding the truth of the relationship in favor of satiating her emotional memory wounds. Until they are made conscious, emotional memory wounds will run Stump's life.

"Now he just needs to propose," Stump thought, "which he might even do tonight!" She imagined the look on his face when he got down on one knee. He would look deep into her bark, with tears in his beautiful eyes... so overtaken with love that he will barely be able to get the words out. "Stump, will you marry me?" "Yes, Boy, I will marry you..."

I know some readers are thinking, "There's NO WAY ANYONE would be this delusional! But, yes, sadly, they are. Remember: it's not their logic talking, but their subconscious emotional woundedness.

Never had Stump been more certain of anything... and never had she felt such unadulterated wholeness and peace in her heart than she did in that moment... with Boy carving her into a toilet.

When emotional memory and trauma bonding fire together, there's no telling how twisted a victim's delusions will get. Astonishingly, the delusions feel incredibly real. Read through this paragraph one more time. Pay attention to Stump's deluded suppositions and rationalizations. Then ask yourself:

1) What information is she selectively forgetting while forming her fantasy?

2) She knows how Boy really is... so why would she intentionally set herself up for the inevitable fall that's he ultimately will bring?

3) HOW is carving her into a toilet - with the intention of crapping in it - showing Stump love? What web of lies must she tell herself to reach this horrific conclusion?

In her current neuro-biologically hijacked and hormonally-flooded state, her fantastical suppositions and rationalizations make perfect sense (to her.) This is how far our emotional memory wounds can bend the minds, hearts, neurons, and souls of otherwise sane and rational people and turn them into prisoners within their own lives.

How exciting! Everything she put on her vision board last year was finally coming true!

Peeps- get this: vision boards – along with every conceivable Law of Attraction trick – and believe me- while in my pit of hell, I tried them ALL – DO NOT, CANNOT, WILL NOT WORK until you are well anchored in your free from the effects of your all-consuming narcissist. First of all, whatever good you are able to generate in your life will immediately get sucked into his black hole. Secondly, without being fully PRESENT in your true self, the universe has no idea "where" to deliver your goods.

And hey; while we're on the subject of ethereal manifestation, that psychic you're giving so much money to? If she is telling you you're destined to be with the guy who has treated you in any way that mimics how Boy is treating Stump – well, she's grossly incorrect. What's happening is this: she has psychically "honed in" on your emotional woundedness and is reflecting back to you what you subconsciously believe you need to heal. Especially, this is for my readers who have been **ghosted** *by a romantic partner and are drowning in grief, and are constantly checking in with their psychic to figure out what's going on. This concept needs a lot more attention than I can give it here. For now, suspend all the ethereal scramblings and give yourself a dose of here-and-now reality. The process of healing your life requires due diligence, and a well-constructed and purposeful abuse recovery program. Once you finally get yourself and your life back, create your vision boards – and they will actually work. You probably won't need your psychic, but, once this has transformed, she won't perpetuate your cycles of abuse if you talk to her.*

The *being carved into a toilet* piece was definitely a surprise, but Almighty God works in mysterious ways!

Wait… what is that passage in the bible again? Oh yeah:

> "And the man shall love thy woman so much that he shall forsake all logic and caring and, for thy own benefit and glee, carve thy precious woman into a receptacle to dump thy shitteth that doth not stinketh anyway-eth, and she shalt give gratitude and wipeth thy asseth with her own wood chips… ith."

No, Stump, that's not a thing. God has nothing to do with this one.

This is the kind of love that Boy's soul needed to melt the icy walls he had built around his sad heart.

*(CogDis) Dear God, Sister Stump! No! Only God (Divine, Tao, Mother Nature, etc… fill in whomever or whatever represents the Divine for you) is powerful enough to deliver the **love** (which sometimes comes in the form of consequence) required to bend the will of the narcissist. What Stump is giving Boy is NOT, in any way, unconditional love. Rather, it is a desperate attempt to garner love, fueled by her unrecognized emotional pain. This is a love imposter, in every way.*

If this meant Stump needed to show him how much she loved him by letting him carve her into a toilet, then by-golly! That's exactly what she would do! Willingly. Enthusiastically. Selflessly. *Carve away, my beautiful Boy! Carve away! For **this** is how much I love you!*

How much delusional irony is in this thought stream? Going for three strikes here:

STRIKE ONE: For starters, let's just focus on the first three words of her ridiculousness: "If this meant…" With "this" being the fact that

"Boy's soul needed unconditional love to melt the icy walls he had built around his heart." But personal sacrifice and debasement is absolutely not an expression or an extension of unconditional love - ESPECIALLY not the kind that Boy needs to "save his soul." Complete delusion - the kind that can lead her to make some really bad, really damaging decisions.

STRIKE TWO: Next, how did Stump come to the conclusion that Boy didn't already know how much she loved him? Of course he did. She's just choosing to ignore the fact that he's exploiting it.

STRIKE THREE: "then by golly! That's exactly what she would do!" Because the first two strikes are so clearly perverse, the foundation of this third strike is also perverse. "Willingly. Selflessly. Enthusiastically" are just fancy adjectives to make her intention sound noble. Really, the more accurate adjectives etc… in this circumstance would be: Delusionally. Irrationally. Catastrophically. Carve away, my deeply disturbed psychopath! Carve away!

Stump's "reality" has been hijacked by her emotional woundedness. Reality is occluded from her conscious thought process. Empaths and codependents often make these types of sweeping rationalizations in order to limp through their horrific situations… all in search of love.

Hours passed. Boy was mostly silent as he worked. No words were needed between them. Stump heard everything he didn't say. She felt his love for her. Her heart was overflowing in love for him.

*She didn't hear anything he didn't say. If she did, she would have heard his monster soul saying, "Nom nom nom nom nom!! Hot damn! What a stupid bitch, letting me carve her into a toilet!" What Stump **really** heard was her own subconscious projections - stemming from her unmet emotional woundedness, which was being temporarily satiated and was thusly flooding her with feel-good hormones… which felt like love.*

And she knew his was for her too.

Um... no, Stump. What you're feeling a temporary satiating of your emotional woundedness.

She could feel it.

Um... NO! Stump's belief that Boy loves her the way she loves him is strictly her own projection of her own woundedness.

In this moment, the world was perfect.

Well... yes - from an emotional-memory standpoint, anyway. Sadly, these moments can't and don't last.

Their bodies fit together perfectly. They were made for each other. She allowed the bliss to overtake her.

Emotional memory will downplay faults and magnify bliss. She "fits together perfectly" with boy on her level of emotional woundedness... and this leads to them fitting together perfectly on the physical level.

She could never explain to anyone why she loved Boy so much, or why she had allowed him to take her apples, her branches, her trunk... her... core.

She could never explain to anyone why she continued to love him so much, or why she had allowed Boy to take her apples, her branches, her trunk... her... core.

Observing a friend or loved one being systematically destroyed, bit-by-bit in real life is just as confounding as it is excruciating. Stump calls this "love." However, the true engine that drives her personal mania is the (many time mentioned now) subconscious wounds of her emotional memory.

Hey! No one needed to understand. It was none of their damn business!

Sweeping rationalization, anyone? Obviously, Stump's actions with Boy are illogical and dysfunctional. No rationalizations, however verbose, intricate, or convicted could possibly satiate the confusion, horror, and disbelief occurring in her friends and family as they watch Boy's creepy, methodical destruction of their beloved. Truth is, at this point, most of them have abandoned ship - the only real way that they could bridge their own cognitive dissonance gaps with the situation.

In all honesty, Stump knew she tolerated a lot from him. In fact, it had gotten to the point that she just no longer told people about how he was treating her, because all they ever did was judge him... or judge her in thinking she was crazy and making it all up.

Here is another example of cognitive dissonance, and a peek into the frustration of trying to "explain" narcissistic abuse to others. It's so outrageous, that, many times, other people don't believe it – even when you try to explain it – which most victims don't.

No one understood their unique relationship. It's just how things needed to be until Boy was able to heal his heart, which could only happen through Stump's persistent and unconditional love.

More delusions... fueled by her hijacked emotional memory. Read through the rest of this section of the story, keeping this in mind.

Now, with him snuggled up to her, carving and smoothing, the waves of pleasure radiating through her roots were quintessential bliss. He was giving her his undivided attention. She knew sacrificing herself for his comfort was exactly what he needed to finally become the man she knew him to be, the man he so desperately wanted to be for her.

She could feel his breath upon her, and, if she closed her eyes and stayed very still, she could feel his heartbeat. THIS moment was a snapshot of true and perfect love... how relationships were meant to be.

Because Stump has never experienced a healthy version of love, she has nothing to compare it to. She has no concrete awareness of Boy's mental pathology or how he wields her unrecognized emotional woundedness - for his own benefit. As is the case with all codependents, her emotional memories have hijacked her life. They are the force behind her grave and terrible relationship decisions and, in essence, are completely "running the show."

Just as the sun was saying its goodnight on the horizon, Boy stood up. "Well, that's done!" His face beamed as he admired his work. "Oh! One more thing..." Boy knelt back down and started carving something into Stump's bark.

"What are you carving into my bark, Boy?" She asked with a sweet giggle. Her voice sounded hollow and without substance. Yet there was joy in her tone.

"Just hold still..." he said reassuringly.

She was excited! She figured he was carving a love poem... to memorialize their deep and abiding connection that had just been magically rekindled... due to her selfless act of kindness and understanding. Perhaps it was a quote that nuanced Stump's unconditional love and forgiveness that she consist-ently and generously showered upon him... a poem that spoke of how they had made it through the fires and tribulations that every healthy relationship goes through. *sigh*... *I just love him so much!*

The delusions get taller on down the line...

"Excellent, excellent..." Boy said with a strange laugh. He stood, stepped back and dusted his hands. "Great! That's done!"

Watch for the strange laugh of the narcissist. Sometimes, it comes out of the blue, and at inappropriate times. The narcissist laugh is becoming known as a telltale indicator. If you listen closely, it's laced with pleasure he derives from his own deviance and evildoings.

Stump felt a combination of relief and sadness at Boy's sudden disengagement. He was done carving... so no more pain. But also... no more of his delicious caresses from smoothing away the wood chips.

This pleasure / pain firing together create the trauma bonding experience.

Surely Boy could feel the love that was just exchanged between them?

Nope, he didn't, Stump. All he feels is the thrill of garnering narcissistic supply from you.

What did all this mean for their relationship?

It means he's done with you — unless you can come up with another way to debase yourself even further for his benefit.

Would he keep his promise to visit her daily?

Not likely.

Would he finally propose marriage?

Ha!

She was counting on her new hollowed-out look to keep him smitten.

Sorry about your delusions, Stump…

"How do I look?" She asked hesitantly.

"Like... a beautiful wooden toilet." Boy answered.

Again, not the compliment she was looking for, but it was something. "Just in time, too. I've got a train pulling into the station that's been choo-choo-choo-ing this whole time!" Boy unbuckled his belt, pulled down his pants, and sat down on Stump. "Whew! Close call!" Pulling a newspaper from his coat pocket, he settled in for a good read.

Boy's brutal neglect of Stump's wellbeing is the move of a narcissist.

Stump suddenly felt confused... and sick. This didn't feel right. In fact, this situation felt really, really... crappy.

It's not right.

This didn't feel good.

It's not good.

This didn't feel like love.

It's not love!

In fact, this situation felt really, really... crappy.

Oh, Dear Stump! How your life would change if you would just go with your instincts – instead of your overarching need to please this heathen!

NO! She mustn't allow herself to think such terrible, selfish thoughts about her poor, emotionally broken, lost and helpless Boy.

YES! Yes, Dear Stump! You MUST allow yourself to think this way... and stop viewing empathy as pity – and a rationalization for allowing yourself to be treated so horribly. If you ever truly wish to heal your life, you must learn to use critical thinking skills! Realize that self-debasement at the request of another is not, in any way, any form, or in any view - LOVE!

She knew he loved her.

How? How do you know he loves you, Stump? If not through his actions, how does one show love? Love must be worked into practical actions and words that serve to support and nurture each other.

And if she could just continue to be compliant, loving, and patient, he would be able to heal from his terrible childhood and finally love her like he truly wanted to, deep inside, and underneath his gruff exterior.

Let's get one thing straight: no one heals from terrible childhoods by being able to commit horrific acts of abuse upon another. In fact, a narcissist can't ever have hopes of healing until their will-of-iron is broken, they hit rock bottom, and they personally adapt an authentic willingness to heal. Maybe one in 100,000 narcissists will reach such a breaking point in their lives. This is up to God - not you. Your job is to heal yourself. You can pray for the narcissist – while simultaneously distancing and PROTECTING yourself from him.

Stump did the right thing: she sat very still, trying to be the best wooden toilet in all the land... so Boy could poop in peace.

"Right thing?" Right for whom? For what? Boy has "trained" Stump to be compliant, while he commits his abuses. In efforts to gain the abuser's approval, victims self-impose radical compliance with even the most heinous of acts. They will dupe themselves into believing that their compliance is an act of love. However, it's not. Calling tolerance of abuse "love" is a blasphemy!

*Also, if it's not yet obvious, Boy pooping into Stump's core is a poignant **metaphor**; narcissists dump their "shit" into their victims, and then blame them for smelling like crap. I know this image is brutal, and probably was difficult to read. But it's no less disgusting or horrifying than what really goes on with narcissists and their victims. I couldn't think of a better way to illustrate it.*

She was very grateful for being able to forgive Boy, and see the bigger picture here. She was a true light-worker!

Um... no. Stump was more like a delusional shit-worker. There is NO virtue – only detriment - in enabling a bully to continue his abuse!

After 20 minutes, Boy folded up his newspaper and tossed it onto the ground. He bent down, picked up a handful of fresh wood chips, wiped his butt and threw them on top of the... steam train steam train that lay at the bottom of the Stump's newly carved hole. He stood up and pulled up his pants. "Well, that feels better!" Plucking his newspaper up from the ground, he said, "Alright, stump! I'm outta here!"

Are we really surprised?

"What??! Wait!" the stump cried. "You're leaving?! Why? I thought..."

Boy's promises are forgotten and denied. His perverse deeds are done, and she has no chance of undoing them. Stump has NOTHING left to offer him. Stump has reached an all-time low.

"Yeah, I gotta get back to Fido."

"You mean... Fella...?"

"Damn it! There you go again, Stump! His name is Fido. I don't know where you got 'Fella.' What a stupid name for a dog-Fella!"

Gaslighting and deflection away from the topic at hand – that he isn't keeping his word to visit her every day...

"But... Boy... I just... we just had such a beautiful time today... and I've done this nice thing here by letting you carve me..."

Boy has NO appreciation for Stump's generosity. He never has and never will. She learned that when he hoarded her apples - without so

"Zip it, Stump! That was a lot-a work I just did for you. My hand is cramped. Besides, you gave me a splinter in my ass. It hurts like a son of a bitch!"

This is the quintessential narcissist: turning his abuse around to "poor me! Poor me! Poor me!" Throwing the blame and a nasty swearword is meant to intimidate, and keep her from fully realizing the unspeakable act of horror that was just committed against her.

Stump was baffled. She was expecting a marriage proposal, after all...

A horrible case of delusion and grave cognitive dissonance...

Boy turned to walk away. He felt indescribably alive. Of course, his joy would fade by the time he reached town, but his life was so depressing, and he always needed to deal with everyone else's bullshit. It was nice to come out on top for a change.

Here we see the brutal, ugly truth about Boy's "payout" for bringing such horrific devastation to Stump: as with her apples, branches, and trunk, the thrill he gets is short lived and minuscule compared to what she's lost. We also see his unjust, paltry rationalizations he uses over what he just did to her – a "friend," and lover, and a good person. Unlike the psychopath, by the way, who behaves in narcissistic ways, people who are narcissists and NOT psychopathic and can feel shades of guilt. This causes them to use outrageous rationalizations to fill the CogDis gap within themselves. With a psychopath, there is absolutely no guilt, and, therefore, no rationalizations are even pondered. It isn't clear from this story which description best fits Boy. In truth, it doesn't much matter to the victim.

In either case, Boy has zero connection to his inner child, his soul, his sense-of-self. These elements are gone. Missing. Nada. Zip. And while this is a call to compassion for those of us who understand the immeasurable pain that would cause a person to become this, this compassion doesn't call for personal debasement or "accepting this as just the way he is." Rather, it's a call to moral outrage, strong boundaries, and a very loud, very resolute, very definitive NO!

"Wait! Boy! What did you carve into my bark?"

"Oh yeah!" He beamed. "I carved a heart... "

"Aw... that's nice, Boy..."

"...with 'Stella & Boy' inside it. I forgot to tell you—I'm getting married."

Behold an example of multi-leveled abuse tactics - considering the argument he and Stump just had about Stella, Fella, Fido, and the boat. His casual response - thrown out as he's walking away — along with "I forgot to tell you!" presents a mishmash of gaslighting, word salad, denial, and about a dozen other narcissistic terms that are yet to be defined by modern society. The fact that Stump know has "Stella and Boy" carved into her trunk is a metaphor for the badges of pain we bear when we continually offer blind forgiveness and unconditional love to an abuser — in a perpetual effort to heal our deepest pain. In spite of the obviousness and all signs pointing to an inevitable conclusion of their relationship of this nature, it ALWAYS comes as a shock to the victim, because they are responding from their inner child, who was initially wounded in the first place.

Stump felt a jolt of the deepest confusion and despair imaginable. *What? How? He was marrying* someone else? But... but... wait... She felt as though she was no longer in her body. She was beside herself. "You're getting married to another woman?!"

The expression, "She was beside herself" is indicative of dissociation – in response to emotional trauma. It nods to cognitive dissonance – she was expecting a marriage proposal; he's marrying someone else.

"Yes, I am." Boy said cheerily.

"But I... but you... but... what about us??!"

"Us? There is no us, Stump." Boy spoke scornfully and dismissively. "You know you and I are just bed buddies."

Even if this was true, being "bed buddies" is based on a mutually beneficial arrangement. Cruelty and degradation of one's "buddy" isn't part of this arrangement - unless, of course, one is narcissistic and he pulls his sleight of language crap. Keep in mind that Boy just said this to a lifelong friend who has given him everything. The opposite of love isn't hate; it's indifference. Him shrugging off her love and reducing it to, "There is no us!" is a perfect example of the essence of narcissism and the core of darkness within it.

"No, Boy! Noooo! You didn't do that to me!"

Of course he did, Stump.

Stump had never felt such utter despair and humiliation.

Boy never felt such triumph and joy.

Narcissists get high on watching other people suffer. It is literally an addiction.

She simply couldn't hold her temper back anymore. "How could you carve another woman's name into my bark? What kind of twisted, cruel, horrible man are you??!" She burst into deep and body-wrenching sobs that echoed to the walls of the hills beyond.

The brutal truth was, in this moment, Stump couldn't possibly grasp the level of cruelty that had just been intentionally committed by Boy. She didn't have the mental framework to understand the level of evil that Boy embodied.

In her mind and heart, Stump genuinely saw the world as a loving, kind place. She knew everyone was good and whole-some at their core, and that love conquers all. What Boy just did made ZERO sense. She scrambled to understand it, but couldn't.

"I'm the twisted, cruel, horrible one? I don't think so!" Boy said coldly. "You're the one who pushed me into another relationship because you constantly were nagging me about seeing another woman!"

Word salad, projection, tangential blame.

"Boooooyyyyy..." she wailed... "I thought... we were so happy, and you should have told me you were marrying another woman... and I let you carve me into a toilet so you would visit me every day..."

"I never said I would visit you every day. I said I could visit you every day, but you're being such a bitch that ain't ever gonna happen now!"

Lying, denial, word salad, projection.

Boy loved arguing semantics. After all, this made him one sexy motherfucker.

Narcissists are so deluded and desperate for attention that they purposely exploit others like this in order to get attention.

"But you're totally acting psycho. Why would I want to visit you?"

Gaslighting, projection, deflection.

"Boy!" Stump yelled. Through gritty tears and the deepest of angst, she spoke as forcefully as she ever had to him. "You promised to visit me every day if I let you carve me into a toilet!!!"

"No, I never said that." He turned his back to her.

Denial.

"Yes you did! You... you... LIAR!!!"

"Liar? Oh, that's real mature. What's next? Are you

gonna tell me my pants are on fire?"

Gaslighting, projection, deflection.

Boy yawned and gazed at the sunset.

Indifference to her pain = gaslighting.

"You see, Stump? This is why you and I would never work. You're just way, way too dramatic for me."

Indifference, word salad, deflection and projection.

Whaaaat? Just... WHAT? How did he turn his nastiness back on her? How could he yawn at a time like this? After what he just did to her?

While Stump's upset is clearly warranted, and her confusion understandable, Boy will never, EVER turn into the wellspring of love she so desperately craves from him. This is stemming, as you know, from her unrecognized childhood woundedness that created this emotional pattern (and subsequent craving) in the first place.

What kind of crazy monster was she dealing with, anyway???

A very dangerous, very vacuous, very deviant monster...

What kind of delusional, crazy-ass monster was she dealing with here?! "What? I'm not dramatic!" Stump shrieked in vain.

What she doesn't get here is that she has the power to reclaim herself. What hurts is facing off with her delusion that Boy isn't the man she thought he was or who she constructed him to be. It's like pulling out the knife: it hurts like hell, but we can't heal the wound if we don't get the knife out.

"Yoouu..." Stump stammered, trying to find words to express her unfathomable pain and anger "You're...you're just a... big... fat... f... fucking... pig... ASSHOLE!!!!"

Even now, it's not too late for Stump to reclaim herself and begin the journey of healing her life. But most victims get caught up in the tornado of desperately trying to "get" the narc to "see" what he's doing, acknowledge her feelings, and step up- into her delusions of who she wants to believe he is.

What? How could Boy laugh at her pain like this?

How could he NOT? His goal is to seek-and-systematically destroy his victim for his own pleasure.

How did he not see how hurt she was? How did he not see that she had given him EVERYTHING that ever meant anything to her – out of the goodness of her heart?

He did see it. He just used it against her.

How could he act so terribly unconcerned about Stump's upset and ungrateful for her stellar generosity?

What Stump sees as "stellar generosity" Boy sees as "opportunity for exploitation."

How could he turn the tables on her and call **her** immature and dramatic? How could he deny that he promised to visit her every day?

Again, how could he NOT, Stump? He's a narcissist. You saw the red flags years ago when he thanklessly took all your apples.

Most importantly, how could he deny their deep and loving soul connection that was so evident in the incredible time they just shared today?

Still, in the face of such clear, empty evilness, Stump is looking for love.

A love that had kept him coming back to her for all these years?

Not only is he missing the empathy chip, his sense-of-self is non-existent. Instead, a black hole of desperation and neediness resides at the core of him — where his soul once dwelled. His ability to garner Stump's life force energy (a.k.a.: soul) temporarily feeds his black-hole-ness.

Stump had no answers, only deep, all-consuming grief... and a sense of a complete obliteration of her sense of self.

Yep, pretty much. This is always a narcissist's goal.

"Boy, don't do this to me..." Stump's desperate tone turned to one of deep mourning. "I love you, Boy. Don't leave."

Desperation is usually the default position for a victim, and deeply rewarding to the narcissist. It's a perfect opportunity to deliver another devastating blow, knowing she won't have any recourse.

"God! You are one crazy bitch!" He chuckled his wicked chuckle again.

Chuckling = pretending to be oblivious to and uninterested in her pain. In fact, Boy finds Stump's pain amusing. A narcissist often accuses his victim of being "crazy" or "out of her mind" because this is exactly his goal – to make her crazy and drive her out of her mind.

"You're out of your mind! A minute ago you were screaming, calling me a pig's asshole."

Here we witness a subtle sleight of language used to deflect and blame. Do you SEE how perversely crazy-making it can be to allow your life to be swept into the black hole of narcissism? Do you understand that this is a gravely mentally sick psychological thriller in which he is the psychotic hunter and you are his prey? YOU can stop this cycle. You can take the reins back on your life. If there's a breath in your body, it's not too late. There are ways to stop this madness and just allow him to be in his empty, pathetic, rotting existence. There are ways for you to rebuild, heal, and thrive. But none of it will work until you drop the notion that your salvation lies in his approval and love. It doesn't. It can't. It never, ever has. And it never, ever will.

"I know... but... but I didn't mean it..." Stump spoke

through her sobs. "I'm just confused…"

Sadly, Stump is confused because of Boy's mental abuse, and not due to her own, organic psychological functioning.

"Oh for fuck's sake! Figure it out. And grow up!"

Here we see the ultimate word salad, deflection, and projection. Besides the stark lack of compassion, he purposefully invoked this scrambled, desperate state in Stump, and then shuns her, viciously faults her for it, and then tells her she's the one who needs to grow up.

Stump felt an eerie darkness overtake her. Boy was walking away, taking with him everything she used to be. Her very core. Her identity. Her soul. And if that wasn't painful enough, in that blessed place where her soul once dwelled, he had dumped a giant, smelly turd.

*This eerie darkness is the inability to fill the cognitive dissonance gap. Confusion, despair, surrender is the result, and is the start of what is colloquially referred to as a **mental breakdown**.*

"Oh! Hey, Stump?" Boy stopped and turned to look at her, as if he had something very important to say. "I just figured something out."

"Wwwhhat… Boy?" She could barely eek out her words. Her muggy thoughts were spinning in non-sensical jargon, in her desperate attempts to process what Boy had just done to her. Now he had some-thing to say to her. What would it be?

*Stump still doesn't "get" that Boy **doesn't love her**, there is no magical fairytale ending, and that he is, in no way, the Prince Charming that her emotional woundedness made him out to be. He's not a good guy. At all. There isn't a teddy bear underneath his gruff exterior. There is a primitive, self-serving lizard. He's not a diamond in the rough. He's a starving monster in the rough — and he's set on destroying her.*

Was he finally understanding how deeply hurt she was?

No.

How wholly devastated she felt in this moment?

Not remotely.

Surely, he must care - even a little bit?

Nope. Not a bit.

Perhaps this was the moment he would confess his true feelings of love for her?

Not a damn chance.

The moment he would make everything right between them?

Nooooo-uh!!

Perhaps this was the moment he would apologize for being so awful to her all these years?

No no no no no!

Perhaps this was the moment he would exonerate her confusion and pain and thank her for always being there for him.

Not gonna happen.

Perhaps Boy was ready to profess his undying love and deep appreciation for the wonderful person Stump had been to him all their lives.

Nope, he won't!

Even if he were to deftly allude to any of this, it would ease her pain tremendously. Stump's life hung in the valance as she breathlessly waited for Boy's parting words.

Notice that even in the face of such bleakness, a victim holds on to shards of hope. Think of this as her "offering up" what's left of her soul for the narcissist to devour. She does this because she mistakenly believes that her salvation rests solely with Boy. She won't say this. She won't even think it. But she will emulate it. And that's enough.

"You really are full of shit." Then Boy, feeling MOST clever for his quick-witted double entendre, laughed an eerie laugh.

Again, the laugh translates to indifference to her pain.

Stump had no rebuttal. She just watched as the love of her life turned his back once more and slowly disappeared into the sunset. She never saw him again.

He's not the love of her life. He's the thief of her soul.

And she lived hollowly ever after.

The End

The end indeed... of Stump's life as she knows it. The place that Stump is in right here, at the end of this harrowing story, is absolutely the setting of suicidal ideation. It may take hours, days, weeks, months, years, but, without intervention and awareness, and with no spiritual essence left (a.k.a.: soul) life in the physical body is excruciating, as it brings about unrelenting cognitive dissonance. This is experienced as extreme anxiety and an unrelenting urge to close the CogDis gap.

The attempt to close this CogDis gap plays out in one of two ways:

1) Obsession and stalking of the narcissist - as she subconsciously is driven to get her soul back" from him.

2) Taking her own life - as she feels completely dead inside.

This isn't difficult to grasp if you think of the narcissist's false self as a mask over a huge, powerful, deep, dark black hole. You get too near it, your soul and all things good and wholesome in your life will get sucked into it. The only power against it is knowledge, healing your own inner woundedness, and up-leveling your existence to a higher vibration that will no longer attract the sharks. Err... the narcs.

If you or a loved one is feeling suicidal or if you work in the mental health field, you must understand this: a person who is suicidal has very likely been narcissistically abused.

Beware that psychotropic medication can exacerbate anxiety as long-buried emotional wounds can be kicked up to the surface. A sense of hopelessness ensues. This is partially why these medications can lead to suicidal ideation in some people, but not in others.

Indeed, loving Soul, share thy
apples, but do so wisely.

Dear Reader,

Before I write anything else in closing, I want to remind you of this: most people are NOT narcissists! You may be on hyper-alert after reading this book, and overly diagnosing narcissism in your family and social circles.

This being said, there are enough narcs in the world to assume that you've run into a few of them over the years. So as much as I don't want you wildly diagnosing narcissism, do not downplay your experiences either.

The process of reading this book may have been as grueling for you as was writing it for me. However, also like me, perhaps the discomfort was worth it. By reading The Giving Stump, your eyes have been opened. Now, you are able to recognize (and, therefore, protect yourself from) narcissistic abuse. As angry as you may feel, please don't confront a narcissist. I've tried, many times over – before knowing any better - and it's never worked out well for me. I've been punched, spit on, verbally threatened and physically assaulted. I've had multiple objects hurled in my direction with the intention of seriously injuring me. I've been insulted, blamed, ridiculed, debased, and demonized in efforts to get me to fall back into the submissive position and relinquish my newfound solvency. I've been accused of being bi-polar, psychotic, and mentally ill – for speaking my truth. I've needed to call the police for my own protection a few times– from people I believed loved me.

*While terrible and frightening to experience, I see that I have healed to such a core level that none of these intimidation tactics were able to shake me from my truth – OR force me back into my default fawning position. It's NOT easy – this path. But it is worth it. I now see other people's awful behavior as reflections, showing me what needs to be healed and transformed within **me** - not within them. This is much different than blaming myself for their behavior. This will be discussed in more detail in the second book in this series: The Surviving Stump.*

*No matter what, do NOT make your goal to **get even** with a narcissist, or even try to talk sense into him. That would be as practical and doable as getting "even" with gravity for causing you to fall and hurt yourself. The fact is, people who behave narcissistically are dealing with emotional and physical trauma untold – and, in spite of appearances, they are actually miserable. This isn't a call to enabling them, but to healing YOU, forgiving them, and, ultimately, transcending what they've come to teach you. In any case, it's not up to you to compromise your own principles, soul, or life force in order to make another person behave a certain way. This is especially true if that person is unwilling to do any personal work to heal his or her own life.*

In fact, any effort you make in trying to "help" (especially if you haven't healed your own stuff) will only feed his or her pathology and allow him or her to further manipulate you. Instead, set out to educate yourself and investigate your subconscious woundedness. Embrace the knowing that you are, indeed, willing and able to do the work necessary to heal and transform your life. You would have never found this book – much less made it through it if you weren't.

Please remember that growth comes through pain. Awareness comes from our assimilation of truth. However grueling your experience was in reading it, I'm hopeful that The Giving Stump has shown you the truth

Thank you for allowing me to be a part of your journey. I am honored more than you could ever know.

Laurel Lee

Self-Awareness: Color and Contemplation

Color the picture of the apple tree below. Contemplate her beauty, her deep green leaves, her solid branches, her life-bearing trunk, her deep roots in Mother Earth, her joy, her life force energy. How does this lovely tree live her most honorable life? How does she best serve humanity? How does she best honor all of life?

Gaze upon me
Bring to thee
The truth of you:
Alive and free!

Self-Awareness: Contemplation and Journal

Contemplate your life, your truth, your potential, your unique gifts and talents, your true moral fiber. How can you live your most honorable life? How do you best serve humanity? How do you best honor God? (the Divine, the Universe, Mother Nature etc...)

Recommended Resources:

thegivingstump.com – for stump-worthy resources and support

melanietoniaevans.com: Narcissistic Abuse Recovery Program

spartanlifecoach.com: Richard Grannon: learn emotional literacy

tm.org: Learn Transcendental Meditation

queenbeeing.com: Discover, Understand, Overcome narc abuse

thetappingsolution.com: Learn Emotional Freedom Technique

omegavector.org: A free personal growth program in Arizona, USA

suicidepreventionlifeline.org: 1-800-273-8255 TTY: 800-799-4889

drsha.com: Soul Healing with Dr. and Master Zhi Gang Sha

#thegivingstump

Deepest Gratitude

to the late Shel Silverstein - the author of The Giving Tree. May The Giving Stump make very clear the meaning of the storyline you wrote over a half-century ago. I honor you.

to Melanie Tonia Evans: for your wisdom, faith and light that you so freely share with others. For your life-saving **Narcissistic Abuse Recovery Program** *which has been a vital key to my healing process. Humanity is absolutely benefiting from the transformational power of your genius!*

to Richard Grannon: for your sheer audacity and ruthless honesty. For the eloquent way you consistently punch narcissism right in the face. For being a solid voice of reason and rebuttal against the pervasive and formidable untruths that have plagued too many of us for far too long.

to my countless teachers, healers, and even, in a weird way, my abusers; without you, I could not have spiritually transformed to the level I have - and this book would not exist.

to Dr. and Master Zhi Gang Sha: for saving my soul when I was drowning in spiritual sludge. I'm thankful beyond words for your sacred wisdom, life-saving blessings, and pure, unconditional love. Please know that I'm not lost; I just need to do this.

A Laurel Production